FOUR TAXIS
FACING NORTH

ALSO BY ELIZABETH WALCOTT-HACKSHAW

Fiction
Mrs B.

Non-fiction: Edited

With Nicole Roberts, Nicole and Elizabeth Walcott-Hackshaw, *Border Crossings: A Trilingual Anthology of Caribbean Women Writers*.

With Martin Munro, *Echoes of the Haitian Revolution: 1804-2004*.

With Martin Munro, *Reinterpreting the Haitian Revolution and its Cultural Aftershocks* (1804-2004).

ELIZABETH WALCOTT-HACKSHAW

FOUR TAXIS
FACING NORTH

SHORT STORIES

PEEPAL TREE

First published in Great Britain in 2007
by Flambard Press
This new edition published in 2017
Peepal Tree Press Ltd
17 King's Avenue
Leeds LS6 1QS
England

ISBN13: 9781845233471

This is a work of fiction. All the characters
appearing in the stories are fictitious.
Any resemblance to real persons,
living or dead, is purely coincidental

Supported using public funding by
ARTS COUNCIL
ENGLAND

CONTENTS

INTRODUCTION

Elizabeth Walcott-Hackshaw's characters are shaped by their pasts. Their fractured lives, created by deceased mothers and departed fathers, dead or missing, pursue her characters and dictate their inner feelings. The terror and violence from without is another source of the fear which eats at their souls and infiltrates the most private moments of their relationships, whether they are parental, with siblings, friends, lovers, or, marital.

This collection belongs to a Caribbean tradition of first-books of childhood and growing up, but is acutely different. It is not at all as you might have come to expect from other collections you may have read. These are manifestly contemporary stories, told in a woman's voice of today, grounded in an understanding of psychology. The tone of these stories is governed by a strong voice. Elizabeth Walcott-Hackshaw is a new voice in Caribbean literature.

If you reflect on the title, *Four Taxis Facing North,* it seems, at first, a simple reference to a quaint, amusing sign seen at a taxi rank in Port of Spain, Trinidad. But it also acts symbolically. It directs us to a vision of a place we may know, and yet, not know enough of, and need to take another look at.

The form or the architecture of each story, through which the narrative unfolds, dictates how we are being led into the plot. It indicates how it digresses, or how the reader is held in anticipation of what is to come. It forces our attention to guess and sympathise. The point of view of each particular narrator is central to our understanding.

For example, a drive out to the country to buy a car in "The

Longest Rope" is charged with the sense that something is going to happen. Something important has already happened and this event is continuing to obsess Katie – though what you thought might be the case is not quite what it seems. This form of telling is done in a straight forward way without any contrived element of craft. The tension is created by being told several stories at the same time. This is analogous to how films work. The writer's achievement is in how various plots are held within a single consciousness, while giving the reader a sense of the lives of others.

In the opening story, "Here", a woman is delayed in a traffic jam at the *carrefour* on the north-east corridor of Trinidad's busy highway with her young daughter, whom she is driving to the airport to send her off to her father in the United States. That is the central narrative. We experience the narrator's inner terror. But there are also the three boys walking along the side of the road, who enter at the opening of the story, and who also preoccupy the narrator. This is another story of terror, which builds to a dark epiphany much later on, throwing a sombre light over the entire plot. Parental stories keep infiltrating the consciousness of the main protagonist: the burying of a father, a mother's three marriages, and the imagined life of the estranged father of her daughter. These preoccupy her, and the reader is dramatically drawn into the lives of these characters as we climb Sans Souci Hill and journey to the airport. Everyday life is vividly described, portraying the island in all its frenetic splendour; the commerce of poverty with its entrepreneurs of deprivation, the Bobo Shantis plying their trade. The three boys are still walking alongside the road into their future, or, maybe not...

These eleven stories can be read as individual texts. Each involves us in the lives of different characters. But they also connect and speak to each other. This is a satisfying, additional quality, amounting to another story, as it were, being told. So, as you read, you experience the reinforcement of different ideas and landscapes through the subtle shifts in point of view. This has the effect of building for the reader a larger picture, with a deeper insight into the drama, the characters and the places that are being explored.

Economy of language and the variety of characters are marked characteristics of this text. There is a fluency that lends an ease to the reading, though, ironically, they are not stories to put us at our ease. They are meant to disturb us, to confront us morally.

The voice of an 'I' narrator, a woman, is the most used point of view. There is one male narrator who tells one story, and even when there is third-person narration, we are in the consciousness of a woman. But these are not stories just for women. Women's stories are never just for women.

Realism is sometimes disturbed by the unusual, as in "The Ward" and "Killing Moons", stories which transport us into a different world, where the illustration is through metaphor and analogies for poverty, alienation and deprivation. The old inimical themes of race and class continue to underlie the modernity and development of contemporary Trinidad.

Throughout, the language is grounded in a clarity whose tone is one you can hear. The stories reflect how people speak, but do not indulge in any cult of dialect. There is wit, irony – and the speaking voices are real. This contributes to an overall authenticity in the collection. Readers can find themselves smiling wryly with the author/narrator. It is clear that this is a world that the writer knows well. Colour, smell, taste, touch and the sounds of the island world are sensuously apprehended, but rendered without any indulgence. Moments of beauty can turn harsh and lead you back to the darker visions of many of these stories. The beauty of place is there, while the inner and outer terror keeps its own pace.

This is a dark Trinidad. It has been remarked that the crime, drug abuse and corruption that form part of everyday life in larger nations become magnified on a small island. Yet this is not merely a collection based on social issues. It is more a map of the heart, expressed without sentimentality.

The title story, "Four Taxis Facing North", gives us the familiar, and yet we realise immediately that we have never seen it in quite this way. Here there is a shift into another genre. This is a visionary story, though here the grounded quality of the real helps the flights of the narrator to remain credible, once you can suspend your disbelief. There is warmth, despite the darkness and there is a love for the place, which you feel might have been destroyed by the experience of several of the narrators. There is a humour and comfort from one who perceives more than we do.

My own favourite story is "The Dolphin's Smile". This is a powerful orchestration of a large number of characters at different times in their lives, in changing locations, living out events which interconnect and shape the lives we are introduced to at *the* event, the funeral, which is the main setting of the story, but, shifting effortlessly as in a film. This quality is part of the contemporariness of this collection. Many moments of the past are marshalled into this one moment to build towards the irrevocable conclusion, which the reader suspects from the beginning, but does not want to happen.

A child's birthday party in "The Party" is another story of entrapment: a woman trapped in a marriage, in a house, in a family, on an island. It is the dry season, a harsh dry season. We all know those moments of preparation for a celebration which seem to be going wrong from the start and the myriad inner and outer occurrences which conspire to create terror in the heart. The dogs have arrived, been put in place for safety, but are not making people safe.

In "Pine Hill" a moral dilemma and a consequential guilt creates a disjuncture in the story. The point of view changes, revealing truths that the characters should realise if they are to continue to live responsibly moral lives in their world, and not be victims of a fear born of prejudice and bigotry. They must act with good judgment. This story offers the greatest possibility of hope, but the protagonists must understand this in order to act. The hope also lies in the writing, in the very language that has been shaped by the author, constructed from a world of paradoxical beauty and fear. This is how the catharsis works.

These are deeply moral stories, but they are not stories with morals. There are no simple lessons or conclusions. They are not religious, though they hint at some of the characters' religious solutions. However, there is a sense in which such solutions are part of the miasma that creates the terror that entraps the characters.

"Four Taxis Facing North" is a strong first book. It is one which I think will find many readers who will want to read and reread these stories. This is a book for general audiences, but it is also a book that will reward multiple readings as a text for study on literature courses in the senior classes of secondary schools and at universities. I can imagine it playing a central part on a course of gender studies. But it is the humanity that underpins each of these stories that brings me to recommend this collection to all readers.

Lawrence Scott
London, 2016

HERE

There are so many cars ahead of me, even today, Saturday, it'll be a while before I get the green light and cross the major intersection, so I look to the left for no reason in particular, and I see three boys walking along the side of the highway; the first in what I call cowman boots, black rubber boots, like the ones I wore as a child so that I could pretend to be the man who took care of the cows opposite our first house in the valley; the second boy taller, skinnier, in rubber slippers, his thin tee-shirt billowing in the wind like a sail; the third with blue-black madras skin in torn khaki shorts and an oversized white vest, and all three powdered with fine, white sand. They skin and grin, all the while staying in their single file, Indian file, one behind the other, on their side of the highway, the side with the coconut trees, the wooden huts, the razor grass, the rice grass, and everything so green except for the white mosque, crescent moon and star rising out of the water with the billboard: *Islam, The Fastest Growing Religion In The World.*

On the other side of the highway is the huge milk factory. Outside its tall gates are pyramids of oranges and grapefruit, piles of mangoes and three old, rusty vans full of gutted kingfish, red fish or carite, with bouquets of blue crabs tied to bamboo sticks planted in ice buckets in the vans' trays. In the middle of the highway, lanes of cars move on either side of the embankment like snails towards or away from the sky-high traffic lights against a cloudless, empty blue sky. At this, the major intersection, this *carrefour,* east, west, north and south converge; trucks, tractors, men at work who are forever widening the road, digging holes, filling holes, only to dig and fill all over again. They've been fixing this highway since I was a child.

The boys pass me; the traffic moves and I catch up to them, then they pass me again. They look so light and free, covered with layers of smells from the cars, the trucks, the factory, the fish, the oranges, the pond, and they laugh and chat, as though they have pockets full of 'blues', one-hundred-dollar-bill-blues, silver shoes, and a view of the ocean from their mansion on the hill.

As I get closer to the lights, the vendors begin to swarm. Timing the lights perfectly, they weave between the crawling cars with bags of oranges, limes, corn, pimentos; weigh pawpaws and pineapples in either hand; roll bins of coconut water, Coca-Cola, bottled water or Apple-J; open black boxes of fake gold watchbands, fake gold watches, knives; haul huge market sacks full of small brown paper bags of cashews, peanuts (salt or fresh), or carry nut cakes wrapped and stacked in huge plastic bags. Rain or shine, there is always the Nut Cake Man with the bandana, hat shades and the strong wrestler's body, the Knife Boy, slim, sharp, six-foot-four, wearing a furry Kangol cap and selling made-in-China knives, and dozens of neatly dressed Bobo Shantis selling nuts from their cotton satchels, and wearing long-sleeved shirts buttoned, tucked and belted into pleated pants, and Baptist blue or red, gold and green Irie cloths wrapped carefully around their dreadlocks.

At the lights before this main intersection there are no vendors, only beggars with twisted arms, back-to-front elbows, limps and jagged bodies, and an elderly Indian couple who walk to beg together. My windows are always rolled up, air-conditioner on, radio on; I know what they look like, how they move, but as they tap on the glass, I just shake my head, sometimes an irritated 'no', sometimes a 'no thanks', sometimes just a flick of the wrist like shooing away flies. It all depends on my day.

But these boys, I've never seen them before. The tallest one, with the cowman boots, is the leader, he must be sixteen or seventeen, maybe even more, perhaps much older than the others, maybe even an uncle (in those families, things like that happen, mother and daughter only fourteen years apart, father and son sixteen, uncles and nephews the same age). The shortest one could be his sister's son; things like that happen in those families, things like that happen all the time here.

They're eating nuts when they pass me again. A Bobo Shanti must have given a bag to them for free because he knows that even though they skin and grin, on the inside, like the inside of their hollow, broken homes, they are mashed up, hungry, molested and abused. They toss the nuts from the brown paper bags into their half-open mouths and the shells flutter in the breeze like tiny butterflies.

She's asleep in the back seat, never makes it to the traffic light on a normal day, far less on one like today. This morning, while I was dressing her, she asked me, 'How long, Mummy? How long?' – and she put up both hands for me to show her, and counting her tiny four-year-old fingers, I say, 'Ten days,' as though ten days were like two and not a lifetime when she is away from me.

The man in the car next to me is staring. I feel sorry for him, for his ugliness, for his inability to see how ugly he is or how people either take pity on him or are irritated by him because he reminds them of some ugliness they may have. I give him a quick smile because that's my mood today, and that smile is meant to say, I feel sorry for your physical appearance, your God-given looks, your curse, now leave me alone.

Everyday the same route, the same traffic, even on a Saturday. I look at my watch and the clock on my dashboard, turn the radio on, then off, check the time again, see if my watch matches the clock, then I do it all again and again, because getting from one light to another can sometimes take a lifetime. This morning she wanted to look at those noisy cartoons; she pleaded, begged, 'Cartoons, Mummy, please,' one billion times, and I always give in, here's your damn cartoon, turn on the TV, keep the room dark. I didn't want to start a day I had been dreading for months. And I have lied to her so many times (as I will again and again because without the lies, it's just too hard), it's not ten days, ten little four-year-old-finger-days, but two months. A lie of the imagination to create a want, a need, a wish; I wish she didn't have to go. My answer to her 'How long, Mummy? How long?' wasn't really a lie but, as I prefer to call it, an imagined truth.

He wants her for the entire summer – two months, ten days, there's no real difference to a four year old, all it is is is time away from Mummy, a lot of time on bad days, but a minute when her daddy gives her everything she wants.

As we inch on, the three boys plant themselves on the pavement at the intersection. I know their story now, they are definitely family, the eldest one is the presumed, appointed leader, the middle one barely a presence, but the third one, because he is the smallest, the apparent follower, will be the most powerful.

At the airport she didn't even realize what happened. I told her she missed the flight, even though we were there two hours before. She even met the flight attendant, pretty with polished, slicked hair, Jackie, Chanel No 5 Jackie, all set to take her from me to him. I hope she doesn't remember all of this, especially Jackie, or breakfast upstairs in that ice box, stinking of frying bacon, fly and cockroach spray (Flit or Baygon?), plane fuel, perfume and black coffee. She wasn't even cold, though dressed only in her jeans, small white Gap top, and Power Puff Girls pink socks and sneakers. Her knapsack held her tiny sweater, her doll Dolly, her notepad and pencils, all set to fly to her daddy. Since she turned four, he's been asking me to send her for a few days, then a week, now two months. I had them all on my side in the beginning, with my stories about his family, the drugs he did in college, the young cousin who had guns under the front seat of his car, the alcoholic aunt, and the repeated hints about their dry-cleaning shops laundering more money than dirty clothes. But perhaps the best thing for my case was the way he just walked out, like a deserter, a coward, abandoning me and our little girl. Maybe that was why the letters between lawyers kept going back and forth and why the judge let me keep her until now.

A father bringing up a little girl is not right, I keep telling my lawyer, Cathy, but all she ever says these days is that he has a right to have her for the two months. That's when I usually hint about his drinking (although he seldom drinks) and that he almost hit me a couple times (he has *almost* hit me but I have always hit him). Cathy usually pretends not to hear; she knows these are my imagined truths, so she just repeats what the judge has decided. But I think of my baby in Miami and how she will be treated because, although she looks light-skinned here, in America she will be black and will have to suffer in ways she would never have to here. Two months will become two years, and then he will take her away from me entirely and I will be the one begging for time. Again, Cathy, my broken record, comes to mind with her 'Judge blah, blah, blah'. As soon as I get to a phone I'm going to fire her, I'm sick of all her speeches. I'll find someone else, a lawyer with a child, preferably a young daughter, because a woman without a child cannot possibly understand the endless horrific possibilities: Tina dead in a car crash, Tina kidnapped, Tina kidnapped and sold to child pornographers, or Tina lost, simply lost in one of those gigantic Miami malls.

I cannot go home for the rest of the day, but where do I take her? The flight, direct to Miami, is only four hours. He'll be waiting, pacing, checking the flight information, thinking she got on another flight, another airline. But then, I would have called him. Confused, speeding thoughts attack his naturally calm, steady mind. Then it'll begin. The calls to Trinidad from the airline office in Miami, calls to Cathy, to everyone I know. How long will it all take before he realizes what I have done? One hour? Maybe two? In a crisis, time is not the same, there are gaps, pauses, rushing ahead (like these damn traffic lights), always a checking of the watch. The airline people will be nice to him; everyone is always so nice to him. Charming, they say, but not in a slick way; he has honest, gentle looks, a gentle man, for all his charm and the fact that although coloured and Trinidadian he looks like a white, Cuban, anti-Castro supporter with a slight tan. For his looks, more than anything else, those Americans will help him.

On the drive to the airport this morning, I went over Sans Souci Hill (how does that translate? Without a Worry Hill? Carefree

Hill?), foolish name for a place where all the residents can barely make ends meet, where most of the young men have no jobs and spend most of the day playing basketball and smoking *zeb,* but she looked so still in the back seat, lying peacefully, eyes closed softly, motionless, hardly a breath. They say that the easiest way to avoid the pain and shock of an accident is to be asleep. Driving over that hill (although I am quite convinced that I could never do it), I have often thought of what it would be like to drive over the edge, straight over the edge; sometimes, I see the car sailing over the valley to another hill or sometimes being held up by the vines that wrap themselves around the heads of the giant trees that grow up from the valley below.

I was his excuse for leaving but he always wanted to go, to Miami, anywhere to get away from us, me, everyone, everything but our Tina. He never liked it here. He didn't want the family, the family business, he didn't want anything to do with home. He left right after we buried my father. That day, supposedly one of the hardest in any life, was much easier than I expected mainly because I was so hungry; I had starved myself for weeks, hoping that denying myself food would make my father stronger. So at the church service, I felt faint, and by the time we got to the cemetery, all I could think about was food. It rained a light thin rain, a funeral rain. Some people had opened their black umbrellas, making it difficult to pass the floral arrangements from the top of the hearse, over the heads of the nuns, in between my father's two spinster sisters, Auntie May and Auntie Winifred, through the rest of the family and friends, to the side of the grave. Everyone came, everyone except my mother. The prayers went on and on, but the hum of the Holy Marys couldn't cover the thuds of the gravediggers throwing heavy clods of damp soil on my father's coffin. He held me and I felt even dizzier because I was so hungry, and the grave, with the candles planted on the moist, dark brown dirt, looked like a delicious chocolate birthday cake.

Father – the word is relative (no pun intended) – my 'real' father, my biological father, never really got to know me or even hold me (according to my mother) because she left him, or he left her, before I was six months old. The reasons have varied throughout the years; there have been tales of infidelity, illness, mental illness, abuse, alcohol, but I know that the true reason is probably all and none of these and perhaps just like him (my estranged husband, whose name I refuse to mention), my father didn't like it here. He came back home to be buried, and maybe my soon-to-be-ex will do that too.

This morning, driving to the airport, driving over Sans Souci in the dark, I kept thinking about driving over the edge and wondering how I would react at exactly that moment when I knew I had finally done it, gone off the road, into the tops of the trees. I could only pray that I wouldn't suddenly panic, that I would be calm, not wake her and hope she would just sleep through it all.

She's waking up; no, just turning. I'll need to explain what happened at the airport in a way that will make four-year-old sense, in a way she can repeat in front of her daddy, or my new lawyer (I have, at least mentally, already fired Cathy). I could say that daddy changed his mind, which would not be a complete lie, since he has changed his mind many times, even about having his now beloved Tina. In the beginning, he thought it was my trap, to force him to marry me, to force him to stay here. But in the end he gave in; the 'why' of it I can only explain by the nature of the gentle beast who would have felt it was the right thing to do, or maybe he knew it was only a temporary measure, a temporary delay, and in three years he would be out. He left us, walked out of the house, just after her third birthday, but he was never really there in the first place.

I am sure he is not alone, although I have no proof, and my Miami spies have only ever seen him with other guys or his old aunts or sisters who fly up to shop in those island-size malls, but I still feel he has someone. A blond Miss Miami whose Cuban parents don't know he has a sister who is darker than I am, with frizzier hair, or a Mandingo Indian uncle. But Miss Miami's parents don't ask, all they see is his charm and his money. They want the marriage, his boat, and the property he will inherit from his father. He will introduce our little girl to Miss Miami who will complement him and enhance his powers to charm others, because she is magazine-pretty, and America rewards such possessions. Tina will worship her and will soon want to look like her and act like her, walk and talk like her. And even though I have no proof of a Miss Miami, I know he cannot be alone; he needs someone to run his home, to take care of his dry cleaning and of my Tina.

My mother married four times. She always says three; that the first one didn't count, whatever that means. Her friends call her the Elizabeth Taylor of the Caribbean. My biological father was her second husband. Sometimes she says she loved him most of all, but for all the reasons (already listed) it didn't work. The other marriages also didn't work because it is hard, according to my mother, to bring 'stepchildren' into a marriage. She tries to sound philosophical, general, generic, but she really means a stepchild, me. But strangely enough, those stepfathers were kinder to me than my own father who just left a space, a hole, a book full of blank pages to fill with imagined days spent together.

My mother loves the idea of marriage, and she glowed when I brought him home. It was a rare moment of praise for me, she was so proud that I had been able to attract, let alone marry, someone like him. 'Startling good looks,' she said. 'Good-looking' was never something she said about me. I learnt from her that all that rubbish about being 'beautiful on the inside' has little to do with getting what you want in life. Thank God Tina is pretty and not too dark.

Finally free from all the traffic lights, my breathing gets worse, not better, becoming more and more laboured, the breaths getting shorter and shorter. I need to stop thinking about where we can go. I cannot go home and I don't want to go home; home has never been, never meant, comfort, safety or peace, so I'll keep driving, farther and farther away from the airport, away from him, but not towards a home. I am determined now he will never have her, not for a month, a week or even a day.

In all these homes, my mother's homes, his homes, our home, quarrels replay in my head. During the day, when I am busy at work, I can turn down the volume, but as I get closer to a home, I hear them so clearly that the shouting gives me a headache. Tina and I are not going home; we will drive to the malls, eat at her favourite restaurant, put off all the calls for at least a couple of hours. I just hope he doesn't call my mother in California because even from that distance, she'll be able to find me, find us, before Cathy, or even the police. Will he call the police? Probably not, his family hates scandals, hates attracting attention.

I see an army of *corbeaux* circling in the distance like hundreds of black Vs against a flat blue cloth. We are on the Beetham highway now, home of the national landfill, the dump. As we drive past, the boys who wait at the entrance, barebacked, shredded shorts, soiled, gloved hands, are ready to help you, guide you through the hills of refuse, for a small fee; they seldom wear masks or handkerchiefs to cover their noses; these Beetham tour guides are accustomed to the smells, the maggots, the dead dogs, the brown diapers, the old sinks, fridges and tires; they have grown up in the plywood, milk-box shacks on the other side of the highway, shacks full of dead, rusting cars used to hide in, lime in, screw in or sleep in when the milk box starts to fall apart. A thick grey haze from the fires and burning tires covers that strip of road like a blanket and I drive through as fast as I can.

Heading towards the capital, Port of Spain, I can see the old lighthouse that stands in the middle of the street, now a roundabout. 'There used to be water here,' my mother always said when she was alive, not half-dead as she is now, at least in my thoughts, living in California with her fourth husband. There are no cruise ships today; these floating cities come to this town from Monday to Friday, to this port that tries to hide its ugliness with bougainvillea and alamanda. The cautious tourists walk through the streets of Port of Spain and compare this port, this capital, to others they have seen in the Caribbean, in more beautiful islands with whiter beaches and friendlier locals. The tourists never venture too far away from the lighthouse, they never go lower down the street where there aren't even flowers to hide the thick, black, oily sea filled with ships lying on their side, like dead dogs on the highway. There they would find shanties, standpipes for showers, holes full of crabs, half-naked children, men and women, living no better than those wrecks in that oily sea.

'Let her stay with me,' I said to him over and over before the lawyers took over all of our conversations. And before long, we could only speak in fragments, broken phrases, because each word felt like another splinter.

I drive away from that town, Port of Spain, a name I always loved as a child, linking my little dot to a bigger somewhere, but now the name irritates me, embarrasses me, especially when the cruise ships arrive. No, we don't speak Spanish here, and I'm sure there is nothing here to remind you of your last trip to Spain. I've never been to Spain and this is not Spain's port, Port of Spain, Port of Pain, Sort of Sane.

My old house, I will soon pass one of my old houses where we lived when I was a child, a house that seemed so strong, able to keep it all out, windows shut, doors closed, curtains drawn, until my mother left my father, or my father left my mother, whichever came first. All I remember is that when they left each other, we cleaned that house as we would a dead body (I've never cleaned a dead body, but I imagine they clean it thoroughly). We took everything out, swept, mopped, bleached, 'Ajaxed', 'Cloroxed' and then put all the furniture back in. But then the cleaning stopped. We let it rot; the furniture cracked, dust settled everywhere, white walls turned to grey, and soon the smell of my mother's perfume could no longer cover the layers of dirt and decay. Uncle Michael, her third husband, who seemed like an angel at first, helped us leave that house, bury it, build another one, but then he left her, or she left him, and we started the cleaning all over again.

I cannot take her home. I cannot face all the calls, the long explanations, the accusations. He will win again, find me and keep her. I have no one on my side, no fathers, mothers, sisters – no more money to waste on bad lawyers. I have wasted so much of my life living it in threes: my mother, my father and me; me, myself and I; replacing fathers with more fathers; replacing husbands with more husbands. I was taught that threes were lucky, good, blessed: the Holy Trinity, the Father, Son and Holy Ghost, three times lucky, La Trinité, the Niña, Pinta, Santa Maria, three in one. How can I take her home?

One day, while on vacation, we were in a rented Jeep. Tina was still in my watermelon stomach and he wanted to drive to the Atlantic side of the island to a beach he had heard about at the foot of a hill. We drove for an hour, passing fishing villages along the way. I saw the sign for the bay so he turned off of the highway onto a sunbaked, rocky dirt road and asked if I was okay. The narrow, broken road took us through a thorny brush then suddenly opened onto a wide, dry field full of gigantic cactus with arms bent upwards in praise, holding huge orange and pink flowers in their prickly palms. It was very windy, the air was salty and you could smell the ocean down below. With so much space and the Atlantic on the horizon, it felt like another place, no longer the Caribbean. But then the trail stopped. Suddenly, we had to find our own way down to the beach. He was driving carefully, even caringly, but the Jeep kept bumping up and down over the cracked ground, so he asked again if I was okay, if I wanted to turn back, but I wanted to get to the ocean, the deep, blue, rough Atlantic and soak both Tina and myself in the water. And then as we turned to go down, we came upon a lone hut, a *case en bois*, with huge holes for windows and a space for a doorway. The *case* had a clear view of the ocean. He slowed down. There were three of them inside the room; two men in their underwear sitting on the ground, and a young boy, barebacked, lying on his stomach in torn shorts on an old mattress, rum bottles scattered everywhere.

The three of them, two men and a boy. The three of us. The men never looked up. The boy turned his face to the wall. So we kept driving to the Atlantic Ocean, the ocean, not the Caribbean Sea, without saying a word about the men and the boy, without saying a word about the three of us.

STRANGE FRUIT

At the back of my father's house there is a fruit called a rambutan; it is strange in a beautiful kind of way, small, not quite round, not exactly oval with soft green spikes that curl as they come out of an orange, red and yellow sunset skin. A Rambutan looks like the *shabine* child of a black sea urchin and a red coral, it looks like it should have come from water, not land; a fruit from the sea, or a coral reef. The inside is less spectacular with a thick, rubbery, round pulp, the colour of coconut jelly, around a small seed. The taste does not live up to the promise of such a tantalizing exterior; it is sweet but not as sweet as coconut jelly and some may even describe the sweetness as bland, which wouldn't be far from the truth. My father planted this tree at the back of the house while my brother and I were away at college. By the time we returned, the Rambutan tree was tall and strong. It's been ten years since I returned to this island, my home, and since then I think about leaving all the time. But then this ridiculous, strange fruit comes to mind, this fruit that is not even native to the Caribbean, not even born here. So I have coined the term 'a Rambutan' for someone who leaves their home forever; when you leave your home 'a Rambutan' is what you become, so my mother who left us a long time ago is 'a Rambutan'. And perhaps one day soon I may become one too.

I am walking towards the grocery store when I hear one middle-aged lady ask her friend about the latest kidnap victim on the island. 'Any news on the Martino boy?' 'No, none,' the other lady replies calmly and they keep on walking. When I get into the grocery store that I have only been into once or twice before, a tall, heavy-set, brown-skinned man in shades keeps following me from one aisle to the next. He does this for three aisles. It troubles me a little at first until I realize he is a security guard. Then I begin to wonder whether he is there to protect me or watch me. Am I a potential victim or suspect? I grab the newspapers and throw them into the cart. The headings are no longer about the Martino boy; he has left page one and is now page-four news; page one is usually the latest murder or kidnap victim or murdered kidnapped victim; every day the dailies gave us the new toll of 'Murder Victims for the Year'. The Martino boy was kidnapped a week ago; by now two more people have been snatched, one driving his car in the cane fields in the south of the island, the other outside a fast-food store. None of these victims are from well-known families so they will not last more than a day on the front page. Based on the murder and kidnapping toll, we are now ranked third after Haiti and Jamaica as one of the most violent places in the Caribbean.

On the drive towards the West, in a murderous twelve o'clock sun, I get a red light (thank God that my air-conditioner is working); young men, with dreadlocks or durags hustle sales at the major intersection; on Saturdays they sell mostly car accessories: furry covers for the steering wheels, miniature plastic dogs with bobbing heads to put on the dashboard, or incense spray for the car. Instead of turning left to head home I go straight down the highway to check on my father. I buy groceries for him on a Saturday. This visit, one that I have been doing for the last two years ever since my father sold his car after deciding he no longer needed such an expense, has gotten more difficult in the last couple of months. My father has become a grump, grousing about everything; he has become more intolerant of what he says is this island's desire to stay Third World. Anything can set him off; usually it is something he has read in the newspapers. I have them delivered to the house now since he fell on his last morning walk to buy the papers at the greengrocer's shop on the corner.

★

As I park outside the gate I notice that the lights are still on from the night before. I call out to our two dogs in the yard, Dingo and Yvetty, but there is no sign of them either. The lawn has not been cut in weeks, the hedges are overgrown and the yard smells of dog urine. The outside of the house is my brother Simon's responsibility. Taking care of our father is supposed to be shared by the two of us; but Simon never does his part willingly, he never forgets to let me know how busy he is, or how important his job is, or what it is like having to work so hard and take care of a family. Simon has a lovely young daughter of six, Simone, but a witch of a wife. Maria and I do not get along. We never did, and as we get older I realize that the only kind of relationship we can hope to have is one where we are able to maintain some semblance of civility. Maria tries to control Simon and how Simon spends his weekends, which she doesn't think should include taking care of his father. His weekends are spent with her family, usually at their embarrassingly large beach house.

On Saturday mornings my father sits on the front porch in a clean white tee-shirt and slightly worn khaki shorts reading the newspapers, pretending not to wait for me. I am always amazed at how good he looks for a man of seventy-two. When I walk into the yard he will make a motion to get up to help me with the groceries and I will tell him 'that's OK Dad' and he will sit down again. As I kiss his damp forehead he will say 'good morning princess' and I will go into the kitchen, unpack the groceries, wash his favourite coffee mug, cereal bowl and spoon in the sink, and start to make him a late breakfast of bacon, scrambled eggs and buttered toast. Seeing the empty chair in the porch this morning gives me the same troubled feeling as I had in the grocery store when the guard was following me. When I unlock the front door I close it too hard, it slams shut, and my hope is to hear my father's voice or some sign of movement inside. Dingo comes to the front of the house to greet me but there is still no sound from the inside. 'Good morning!' I say as cheerily as I can. 'Dad!' I say again, this time not as cheerful.

The house feels empty because a house has a life; it can feel alive or too still, it has a different way of breathing or being when people are in it. Even though my instinct tells me he is not here, I am still afraid of what I might find as I walk past our old bedrooms to get to the master bedroom where my parents slept when Simon and I were children. My father still sleeps in that room; he never wanted to move from this house, even after my mother left him. Nothing looks different in the hallway, everything is in its place, the paintings haven't shifted, the beds in all the bedrooms are made, the house does not feel dusty, which means that the housekeeper Patsy came yesterday, Friday, to clean and do extra cooking for the weekend (I pay for Patsy to come in half-day during the week and for a full day on Friday); nothing feels different except this unsettling stillness.

All the other bedrooms, four of them, line the hallway but the master bedroom is at the top of the hall. That door is closed. I am almost sure he is not here but the sight of the closed door makes me feel uneasy once again. Suddenly, the thought of the chicken defrosting in the back seat pops into my head. I should go back and take it out of the hot sun before I open the door; food poisoning, meat going bad, wasting all that money, these are my silly worries as I face the door, knocking three times, still nothing. I open it not gently but hard and it slams against the wall. If there is anything to face inside I want to see it right away. What I find is only part of what I expect; the bed is too neat, too smooth to have been slept in, the newspapers usually stacked neatly in a pile just under the TV stand are scattered on the faded Persian rug in front of the TV. A pair of scissors is on the bedside table with two articles cut from the papers under a glass of water in a white saucer. A black fly floats in the water and ants sketch brown lines across the plate. Over the last year or so my father has developed an obsession with the crime situation on the island, so he cuts out articles from the front page, the editorials, and anything to do with murders, drug busts, and especially kidnappings. He puts the articles in shoeboxes and they sometimes resurface in a scrapbook. I have seen him look at the seven o'clock news broadcast on TV and compare what is said to what is written in the newspapers. It's rare that he doesn't find a discrepancy in the two reports; the carelessness in figures quoted, or even errors in the identification of people and places. He always listens and looks for grammatical errors, circling the mistakes with a red pen in the papers and verbally correcting the talking head on TV. These careless errors, he says, keeps us in the Third World no matter how rich the oil makes the island. I pick up the two articles; one is about the Martino boy who is still missing after a week; the other is about the burial of a headless body, a Professor from the local University, whose body was found in the Valencia forest. After searching for the Professor's head for a week the family decided to go ahead and bury the body. We have all become detectives on the island; we know when it is a drug crime or not; missing heads and fingers are all signs that the victim or the victim's family has a drug connection. The Professor's death has created quite a stir, the reporters feed on it especially since he was a Head of Department at the University. Needless to say the papers had a field day with the headlines, 'Headless Head Found Dead' and 'University Head without a Head'; it went on for days.

My father has always been an extremely neat man so it is strange to see things out of place: articles not filed, glass and saucer next to bed, white tee-shirt and khaki shorts tossed on the *chaise longue* near the small bookcase. I sit on the bed that faces a full- length mirror (my mother, who was and perhaps still is thought to be quite beautiful, loved mirrors and so in this bedroom alone there are three); a quick glance at my face shows all my anxiety. Then the maybes start to run through my mind: maybe he is lying in the bathroom unconscious from a bad fall, maybe he went for an early morning walk and was hit by a car, maybe bandits broke into the house, snatched him and now he is lying bleeding in some forest. The maybes don't stop even after I check the three bathrooms in the house; in each one I open the door hoping not to find him collapsed in the tub or shower. I check the closet for his sneakers (they are there, neatly lined up with his other pairs, nothing seems to be missing, but I'm not sure) and I check the other bedrooms to see if anything is out of place or broken; nothing suggests a struggle or a break-in. At the back of the house as I walk around (maybe he is there and just hadn't heard me calling out to him) I notice that the dogs' bowls are clean, as though they hadn't been fed the night before. Usually on a Saturday morning I would have to wash away the food in and around the bowls. My father does not like dogs and the only reason he has them is because Simon and I insist that he keep them for his own security. After many battles he agreed but would do no more than feed them; vets, baths, and any other kind of dog maintenance activity would be left to us, and that of course means me.

I want to call Simon not only because I am worried but also because I miss Simon and I see this as an opportunity to share something with him, to have him close and attentive to me, at least until we find my father. Walking to the car I suddenly remember a game we used to play in the back seat; Simon would tickle me while my mother drove and I would have to laugh without making a sound (my mother hated it when we screamed or made any loud noises in the car because driving always made her nervous). So it would be a silent, muffled laugh at first and then I would explode, only to face my mother's own scream to keep quiet, followed by a million threats of what would happen if I screamed again. Simon, being the older one, knew when he could get away with our little crimes and when he had to be perfect; he could read my mother's moods like a book. I could not because she moved so quickly between joy and anger or sadness and laughter that I was always on the wrong page with her. My father used to make fun of her, saying she had the most beautiful temper he had ever seen. But like Simon he knew how to pick his moments. At night after we said our prayers with our mother, who always kissed us twice on both cheeks, her breath smelling of red wine and her hair the scent of almonds and vanilla, Simon and I used to play games in the dark. One game was to see who could say that they loved each other the most. I would tell Simon I loved him a million, billion, trillion, zillion etc… and he would do the same until we fell asleep; I truly believed in those days that I would marry Simon. Although we had separate rooms, Simon and I slept in the same room until Simon went to high school at eleven, and even then there would be times when I would sneak into his room or he into mine after our parents had gone to bed.

The eleven o'clock sun is turning the car into a microwave, defrosting all of the meats. As I take the bags out of the back seat, I keep looking down the road hoping to see the tall, slim figure of my father coming towards me. It takes two trips back and forth to the kitchen to bring in all the grocery bags and each time I open the gate I glance down willing him to appear. Back inside I am suddenly very hungry so I have a bowl of muesli with milk. From where I sit on the stairs the phone is within reach but I am nervous about calling Simon. I want to be able to tell him that I have checked everywhere. I don't want to sound like a fool and certainly don't want to get his sympathy for my frazzled state only to see my father reappear. But most of all I don't want to look like a fool in front of Maria. For Simon shares everything with her and this has made it impossible for me to remain close to my brother even though we were very close as children. I was sure then that Simon was going to be my soulmate for life. When my mother began to leave us (because she didn't leave all at once but rather in stages) Simon and I relied on each other more because our father barely spoke to us about her leaving. Simon and I would make up scenarios about how happy we would all be when she came home. It was very lonely when she wasn't around; we missed her laugh and her beautiful smile. But we gave our father the hardest time because the parent that leaves pays later but the one that is left behind pays right away. Once, our father tried to introduce us to some 'Auntie' while our mother was 'away'. Simon and I were so rude the poor lady never came back to the house.

Before I call Simon I decide to check in with Patsy. Her number is on a list of important numbers that I have put on a whiteboard on the fridge door. Patsy is just below THE POLICE and DR PREVATT. One of Patsy's daughters answers the phone; Patsy is at church, Saturday is her church day, but the daughter confirms that Patsy came on Friday; however she cannot say whether Mr John was there. John is my father's first name but they never call him Mr Carter. Patsy will be back from church at two o'clock so I leave my father's phone number (which I am sure Patsy has) and my cell number. Now I have every reason to call Simon. Taking one last look outside, I begin to dial the number.

'Maria, hi, it's Michelle, is Simon around?' There is the usual pause to be followed by the singsong voice that is cultivated by anyone who grew up in Maria's part of the island and went to Maria's high school.

'Hi, Shell, how are you going, we haven't heard from you in such a long time?' All the words go up and down like a seesaw, and already I am irritated; first, because I only like Simon to call me Shell – coming from anyone else it sounds like I belong on a beach – and second she has already begun to correct me in her usual indirect way because I have called and not asked about her welfare, or made the usual inane small talk required before a simple request to speak to my brother. These are small-island manners that Simon and I were never really taught to follow.

'Yeah, work keeps me really busy, listen is Simon there? I really need to talk to him.' My counterattack is quite obvious but may be missed by Maria who is a housewife with a babysitter and a housekeeper and a 'yard boy' of sixty-five, so although she continually complains about how tired she is, I find it hard to believe that she has any work to do, especially since her only daughter is in school. My second weapon is to peak her interest because she always wants to know everything about Simon's life.

'Can I help with anything, Shell?'

'Yes, you can put Simon on the phone.' I try to make the sentence sound lighthearted, but I think my voice is filled with too much anger and anxiety about my father to actually pull it off. There is silence on the other end and I hear my brother's voice as he takes the phone from her.

'Yeah Shell, how goes it?' All the stress of the morning is released when I hear his buoyant voice; my eyes fill with tears but even then I am able to think about the effect these tears will have on Simon. Will he get irritated or rush over to my father's house to console me?

'Not so great Si, I can't find Daddy.'

'What do you mean you can't find him?'

'When I came this morning, well closer to lunch, with the groceries he wasn't here. I've been around the house a million times, I've checked the back, his bed doesn't even look as though someone slept in it.'

'Well, Shell, maybe he had a little night out on the town. The man may be seventy-seven but…'

'First of all he is seventy-two and he has never done something like this.'

'How do you know that? Maybe he has and you just never found out about it. You're not his babysitter, Shell.' This is the Simon I do not like, the one who has to keep everything bouncing lightly on the surface, never wanting to go too far below, afraid of what he might find. So his attacks are tangential, even cheery, but attacks nonetheless.

'OK fine, Simon, as usual I'll handle it, have a nice day, 'and I slam the receiver down.

I wait near to the phone because I know that Simon will call back. It takes a little longer than I expect because I have enough time to notice how tired I look in one of my mother's many mirrors. The dark circles around my eyes have been there for weeks, ever since I started to work in the bookstore and the boss, Mr Singh, gave me all the horrible shifts; I either have to open or close and then I have to get the keys back to him before I get home. This is what a Master's Degree in English Literature at a Private New England University gets me, a sale's-girl position in the fiction section of a local wannabe Barnes and Noble. The phone finally rings and I'm sure that it's Simon but it's not; instead it's Patsy.

'Yes, Miss Carter, I was there on Friday but when I come the door was open and I didn't see your father up 'til I leave at two.'

'But what time you got there in the morning?'

'Usual time, eight.'

'And he wasn't there at eight? You didn't see a note or anything.'

'Mr Carter don't normally leave a note because normally he there to tell me what to do. But up 'til I leave at two on Friday I didn't see no sign of him.'

Patsy doesn't ask, her manners are too good for that, but I can tell that she sounds worried.

'Well, when I hear from my Dad I'll call you, Patsy, thanks for calling back.'

A sudden slam of a door outside makes me jump. 'Dad?' I repeat at least three times before I get to the kitchen and realize that I have forgotten to pull the door in. It's just the wind.

Waiting for Simon to call back proves more difficult than I imagine. I want to pick up the phone and dial to show how serious the situation has become. Our father has been missing for not one but maybe even two days, if what Patsy says is correct. The house is hot, even the huge oil paintings that my mother hung around the dining and living rooms seem to be sweating. I stop to look at the one painting my father bought which my mother always hated and Simon and I loved because it looked like the figure of a fat lady's bottom; its real title was 'Knife with Pear'. They argued about this painting, my mother insisting that it be moved to my father's study but for once my father held his ground with her and refused to give in. We later found out that my mother's hatred of this painting had little to do with my father's bad taste in art, and everything to do with the artist who turned out to be one of my father's 'lady friends'. When I was away at university I always remember the morning when Simon called me up to say that he was staring at 'Fat Lady with Bottom' (the title Simon and I secretly gave to the painting), waiting to drive my mother to the airport. That was the day she left us for good. By now we were used to her leaving; she would go to Barbados, Jamaica or further away like London, New York, Miami or even Paris, spend a week or even a month, and then somehow my father would persuade her to come back. The first time she left, she prepared us with a long tale about shopping for the family and the need to see her publishers; my mother writes children's stories. Her publishers are in New York, but New York was seldom where she went when she left. In the beginning she prepared us for her departure but after a while it took less and less time. And we began to notice a pattern: there would be an argument, she metamorphosed into hurricane Monica ripping through the house, everyone feeling the effects, then there would be a terrible calm and the house would be still and in the stillness she would leave. Sometimes the cycle took a few days, but usually it took a week from cyclone to departure. She finally left for good when I was nineteen, in my sophomore year; Simon was twenty-one and already in the process of setting-up the first of many successful business ventures. He had come home from studying in Canada the year before.

In this heat 'Fat Lady with Bottom' looked as though all the colours were about to melt and drip from the canvas to the couch below. I never liked to admit that I missed my mother but at times like these I wished she were still around to tell us what to do. By now she would have had a plan and made enough calls to know where he wasn't. But unlike my mother I froze in a crisis: barely able to think in complete sentences and when I did have an idea it was usually to call someone to help me figure out my next move. Simon was more like my mother in that way; he acted, he made decisions and he seldom froze, except for that day when he called me about taking her to the airport. He could not explain what was happening except to describe the sunny morning, the painting and the fact that my mother had called him at five a.m. asking him to take her to the airport. My father never came out of the bedroom that morning, and she only had two suitcases; everything seemed as though this was just another Miami/New York publisher/ shopping expedition. But the house did not feel right; it gave away the secret; on the phone Simon said that everything felt too still even though our mother tried to be her chatty self.

From that day we seemed to be allied to different camps: Simon fell into our mother's and I joined my father's army. What did she tell him on the drive to the airport that made him move in a matter of hours from enemy to ally? He never really told me what they spoke about, and what I resented even more was that she called me almost a week later to tell me she had left and was in Miami living with a cousin who had migrated there the year before. It would be easier to get to her publishers in New York from Miami; she never spoke about leaving my father or us for that matter. But the desertion of my father was obvious to me. That Christmas, when I came home to spend it with him, I saw him mourn what seemed like such a vicious act of abandonment. And that Christmas Simon and I had one of our worst fights, mainly because my brother's reading differed so greatly from mine. For Simon, my mother had finally escaped years of living a life that stifled her and forced her to make sacrifices so that she could take care of her family; now that we were adults Simon saw it as her chance to be able finally to live her own life. I had to tell Simon in no uncertain terms that I thought what he said complete and utter crap. When did he start to see our mother as some meek and mild housewife? She had always travelled whenever she wanted, she had found time to write; her *Caribbean Tales* (volumes one and two) and *The Life and Times of Shelly the Snail* had done very well, enough to secure publishers in New York and London. I had admired my mother for her courage not her timidity; she could be fierce, charming, gentle and terribly witty but mild she was not. Simon knew that our mother controlled what we did on weekends, what we ate, who we socialized with, where we went on vacation. After she left I could only see her selfishness and the damage and destruction she left in her path. Whenever my mother had one of her famous temper outbursts my father would say to us, 'Hurricane Monica has just passed, good weather will be here soon.' The good weather in our house had everything to do with my mother, since her mood determined the mood of the house; but she could switch so dramatically, so quickly, that in a matter of minutes her screams could turn into smiles and she could make us all laugh again even after the worst storm.

The realignment of alliances formed after the divorce was

strange because before then it had been the reverse; Simon had always protected our father and our father had always supported Simon, doing everything he could to give him the best education, the best tennis coach on the island, the best French tutor, and neglected to see how self-important Simon was becoming. I adored my mother and set everything I did against her very high standards, whereas my father who never seemed to criticize or even correct me irritated me beyond belief for his lack of ambition and desire to settle for a fameless middle-manager existence. He complained about the way the country was run, he blamed everyone in his own family for his situation, but he never looked at himself.

I was lost in my musings when I suddenly turned and saw Simon standing in the doorway, the dogs hadn't made a sound. The look on his face really worried me.

'What is it, Si?' I could feel myself close to tears now.

'Look, I passed by Patsy's house and she said that she hadn't seen him for the whole day on Friday. By the time she came he had already left, the bed was made and everything.'

'So that means he's been gone since Thursday night?' The tears are falling now even though I am pressing my cheeks, trying to stop the flow. 'But maybe he came back after she left, what time did she say she left?'

'I don't remember. The point is she didn't see him at all, Shell, so that makes it Thursday, Friday and now Saturday.'

'And what about the articles and the cup and saucer. Patsy would have cleaned that up on Friday, and when I came in there was stuff next to the bed...' But before I finish the floodgates open. I see my father being taken from the house by three masked bandits, shoved into a car where he is kicked, hit and slapped and driven to the Valencia forest, where he is put into some hole that they have already dug. I see his terrified face; he is begging, whimpering like a baby, his body is bent and shaking. Simon doesn't move to comfort me. No, he just stands there.

'This is not the time to lose it, Shell.'

'OK, Simon, I'll stop and you can tell me exactly when I can lose it because you seem to know everything, Simon, *you're* the one that comes here every Saturday to see how *our* father is going, *you're* the one who buys the groceries, *you're* the one who calls him every night just to see how his day went...' I start to cry even harder even though I know that Simon is right (he's a self-righteous tight ass) but this is definitely not the time to fall apart or to fall into the same potholes that Simon and I manage to fall into once we start to discuss our parents.

Simon gives me one of his superior stares and then starts to walk around the house like some detective searching for clues. He comes back out with pen and paper and informs me that he is about to make a list of the people we need to call.

'We need to call the police, Uncle Paul, Auntie B, take a walk around the neighbourhood, check the shop to see when he got the newspapers...'

'He doesn't get the papers anymore, I have them delivered, remember.' I say this as sarcastically as I can but Simon doesn't seem to notice. As Simon continues to make his neat list I realize how beautiful he still is. He was born that way and my mother would always introduce him as her gorgeous son: 'Have you met my gorgeous son, Simon?' Sometimes I would be standing close enough to hear the difference in her voice when she turned to me: 'And this is my Michelle.' A possessive adjective would suffice, not a beautiful descriptive one; I was hers, she had borne me. But she looked at Simon in the same way that she admired a painting, with such appreciation and adoration. That was the look she never gave me and yet I worshipped her when we were young.

Simon makes several calls, the first to my father's brother Uncle Paul, just to see, Simon says, if our father is at his house. Uncle Paul is in Texas on business but our Aunt Barbara (who we all call Auntie B) immediately begins to panic, saying she will send our cousin Robert over to help us look for him. She begins to worry that our father has been kidnapped and asks Simon if he has called the police and AKS (Anti-Kidnapping Squad). Auntie B launches into a discussion on how bad things are and the fact that the Martino boy is still missing but she knows that the family is saying prayers everyday for him. Auntie B belongs to the local Opus Dei and goes to Mass everyday. Simon cuts her off politely and says he has called the police and will also make a call to a family friend in the army; the lie is so calm and convincing that even I am impressed. He then assures Auntie B that she does not need to send Robert over, at least not yet. But we both know that she will call Robert immediately and Robert will waste no time in getting to us. If Simon has had a rival in his golden life it has been our cousin Robert. From early on it was clear that either Robert or Simon would be chosen to lead the Carter clan. Ridiculous things like future leaders were still important to our father's family. Simon and Robert were just a year apart, but that year mattered so much; it gave Robert first place in everything. Robert gave the family its first grandchild, its first grandson; Robert was first in his class, first to get a scholarship to Harvard, first to get married, start a business, and the list of firsts never seems to end. And Simon, although admittedly gorgeous, could only ever be a gorgeous second. What was worse Robert had always been able to charm anyone who came along and that included our mother. She could not resist beauty, and Robert, like Simon, was beautiful.

Our mother would have preferred Simon to be the first in the family to achieve Robert's success, and to everyone else Simon was extremely successful, but the only time he fell short was when a comparison was made with Robert. My mother was also powerless before Robert's old-school elegance, something he had obviously learned from Uncle Paul, whom my mother also adored. But typical of my mother and her twisted logic, she shifted the competition from Simon and Robert (a competition Simon could never win) to my father and Uncle Paul. At least at first glance my father was the less attractive, less athletic, less moneyed, less successful of the two Carter brothers, but there was one area where my father definitely beat his brother and that was, in my mother's opinion, in their choice of wives. Who could deny that my mother was not more beautiful, more intelligent, and more cultured than Auntie B? My mother saw herself as my father's only edge at family gatherings. And both Simon and I felt proud to walk into a party with this perfumed, impeccably dressed lady who made everyone look at her and want to talk to her. My mother would position herself next to someone she regarded as an easy opponent who provided an obvious contrast to her own striking good looks; this person was often Auntie B, my mother's antithesis. On the way home my mother would often say to our father, 'I never understood how Paul could marry such a dumpy little lady, so homely.' My father never replied to these acrid remarks, he just let them hover for a moment then fall, hopefully with a soft, quiet landing. He has always liked Auntie B for everything she never tries to be, for the ease with which she moves around, never trying to draw attention to herself, never trying to win an argument. Maybe my father, like me, still wonders at his brother's choice of a wife – his brother who, my father said, only dated beauty queens, local or foreign, when he was younger. I wonder why someone like Auntie B could have married someone like Uncle Paul; perhaps it was for the same strange reason that my father married someone like my mother.

I like my Auntie B a lot but in all honesty, at those large family gatherings, she always did look frumpy compared to my mother, who always looked extremely polished and definitely made an extra effort for this crowd. Auntie B would be in her usual long, sleeveless summer dress, wearing very little make-up and a pair of flat sandals while my mother would be in her crisp white trousers, favourite navy belt, and a tailored white or navy-striped tee-shirt and always wearing her Jackie O shades or perching them perfectly on her shiny, smooth, dark brown hair. Auntie B looked like she was heading for the market, and my mother for her yacht. And when my Uncle Paul kissed me on both my cheeks, he never forgot to tell me how lovely I looked and what a lucky girl I was to have inherited such 'fine bones', then he would inevitably add, 'Genes, you can never beat good genes, eh Johnny?' My father would smile and then try to offer a nice compliment to Auntie B, who always put herself down in some way after being told something nice about her looks, her house, or her cooking. The only time she agreed was when they spoke about Robert; then she would have to agree as much as Auntie B could, 'Yes, thank God, he's doing quite well these days, he's a good businessman like his father.'

Simon hesitates before calling the police and there are many reasons why he should; these days with so many crimes on the island there is always a policeman or an army officer involved. Senior police officers have been linked to several kidnappings, but when it came to their day in court the witnesses often disappeared, or accidentally hanged or shot themselves. We both knew that if our father was not in danger he would be embarrassed to have been reported missing to the police, like some Alzheimer's patient. But we make the call anyway. At least Simon does. In the meantime I make some tuna sandwiches for us. It was always part of my mother's solution for any crisis; to make sure we ate so we could think clearly.

In the last year I have become quite close to my father although I have never asked the questions that haunt me even now. How did he manage to go on even after she left? Why did she leave us? These are things I will never ask. And yet I have become close to him in a very practical way. I call him almost every night; the call usually lasts five minutes unless something special has occurred in the news; this could be a kidnapping in our part of the country, like the Martino boy, or the murder of some businessman we all know. Other than that I call to check that he has eaten, that Patsy came, and that he has locked up the house properly. We seldom go into any personal details or complicated feelings; I always say that I am fine, a little tired, and share some joke about the bookshop owner Mr Singh whose English is amazingly horrible. My father enjoys those jokes.

Simon and I eat in silence and wait for Constable Joseph and Sergeant Roberts to arrive in a small blue and white police vehicle. We are surprised at how soon they get to us. Simon puts the dogs in the kennel at the back of the house, even though he assures them that because we are there the dogs are safe. But they refuse to go beyond the gate; Sergeant Joseph looks ex-

tremely concerned and asks if the dogs 'are secured'. My mater-
nal grandmother, like my mother, had very fair skin and tried
her best to forget 'her touch of tar'; she would always say, 'Black
people don't like black dogs.' Even though my father's family
had a very snobbish attitude towards the uneducated and
unrefined, they never indulged, as my mother's family did, in
gross racial remarks against their own race. I could tell that my
father hated these statements but to keep the peace he said very
little and avoided my mother's mother as much as he could
while she was alive.

Roberts is in plain clothes and Joseph in uniform. All the
policemen on the island have a similar look; Black or Indian, they
smell of Palmolive soap, are razor-clean shaven, have short
square hair cuts and a way of speaking in a half-friendly, half-
officious manner, a tone that always suggests a lack of complete
trust in what is being said to them. And a man's word always
weighs more than a woman's, so even though I am the one who
discovered that my father is missing, they speak mainly to Simon.
This irritates me but I let it go and offer juice, water, or coffee –
they both accept water.

Only Constable Joseph asks the questions; Sergeant Roberts
just looks on and smiles at us in a way that makes me feel very
uncomfortable. There is a feeling of mistrust on both sides.
Simon tells them the sequence of events and every once in a while
I add a little precision to the statement with a time or place.

'How old is your father?' Constable Joseph asks.

Simon hesitates so I say, 'Seventy-two.'

'Does he have a medical condition?'

'No, none. A few years ago he had minor surgery for a hernia,
but that's it I think.' Simon looks at me for confirmation. I nod.

'Has he ever left home like this before?'

'You mean without letting us know where he is going?'

Joseph says, 'Yes, without a call or a note.'

'No, not that I know of,' Simon says.

'Have you tried to contact his friends, neighbours or any other
relatives to see if he may be there?'

'Yes and no. We've called close relatives but we haven't called his friends. He doesn't really have a lot of friends, maybe one or two from his job. But my father is a loner and since his retirement a few years ago he has gotten… he has spent more time alone.'

There is a pause. I can see that Simon feels foolish, as though he is failing a test, unprepared and incompetent, and all of this reflects badly on him and the family. Simon forgets that this is about my father, not Simon, but right now he is focusing on *his* performance.

'Excuse me but I must ask again if your father has any medical condition. Has he ever wandered away from home before?' Constable Joseph says this in a very soft voice but I can tell that he has already begun to get an image of my father that is wrong. He is not some lonely, senile old man who wanders away from home in a white vest, torn khaki shorts and slippers, smelling of urine, mumbling and drooling like a baby. This undignified image irritates me. So I say what I think will erase this image.

'Maybe he is with a lady-friend.'

At this even Simon looks startled. 'What lady-friend are you talking about?'

Both policemen smile. I feel foolish but I continue to insist on what is pure fiction.

'What about Mrs. Gittens, the widower in the next street? Or Shirley from the Tennis Club?'

'That was years ago.' Simon says. 'Our father does not have a girlfriend or a lady-friend. Shell, what are you talking about?' I catch a glimpse of the two police officers exchanging a quick smirk.

'How would you know, Simon? When last did you really ask Daddy how he was?' We both manage to stop ourselves.

The entire situation is embarrassing for my father, for me and for Simon. So I get up from the table in the dining room where the four of us are seated, obviously on the verge of tears, say 'excuse me' and go into the kitchen. Drinking a glass of water does not conceal that I am crying again and feeling extremely exhausted. I got here at eleven this morning and it is now two o'clock – three hours and still no word from my father. There is a great desire on my part to call my mother, if only to make her pay for all the unhappiness she has caused us over the years. I even blame her for this. My aim would be to inflict a guilt that would wound her so terribly that she would feel compelled to come home and leave her beautiful life.

From the kitchen, I hear the tone of the questions differ; they seem kinder. It seems that because we have revealed our fragility and our façade of control and superiority has fallen apart, exposing our weakness and vulnerability, the policeman are ready to show us some mercy. But we have done nothing that we should have; we haven't walked around the neighbourhood, we haven't checked the hospital, we haven't called his friend George who he plays chess with at least once a month. And I hear Simon explaining that my father lives alone our mother lives in New York. In the meantime I answer three calls: one from Auntie B, one from Uncle Paul at the airport in Houston, Texas, and the other from Robert who is on his way. Maria also calls and it's a pleasure to tell her I am on the other line so she will have to call back.

Not once do I hear the policemen even suggest the possibility of my father being kidnapped. This is supposed to comfort me but their refusal even to consider it makes me feel that they do not deem my father worthy of being kidnapped. Are the surroundings too quietly tasteful? The first-edition books my father collects and our mother's paintings don't seem to count for much, nor do her Persian rugs; they do not recognize what is of value. Or is it that my father was just a manager in a small local firm? An administrative job that he did without much effort and little enjoyment but afforded him the time to read and listen to his music on the weekends. During their marriage my mother and father would argue about his not wanting to work in the successful family business, Carter & Co. Uncle Paul became president of the company after Grandpa Carter died. My father had gotten a sizeable inheritance, which he used for our education and to continue to enjoy his middle-class existence. But Uncle Paul, through the company, had managed to acquire some prime real estate on the island and in Miami, and now that we were going through another oil boom, he was doing extremely well renting executive homes to American and British Oil Company executives.

This apparent lack of ambition, my mother theorized, was the result of my father's background; having come from a family that was quite well off, my father never really had to think about money. My mother saw this as a sign of laziness. I may have agreed with her when I was younger but now I see my father differently, a man more at peace with himself than my Uncle Paul or even my mother. Just the thought of my mother at this moment sends me into a quiet rage. The urge is too strong: I reach for the phone and dial the New York number I have somehow committed to memory even though I only speak to my mother twice a month. It rings; my heart races because now I am not quite sure what to say. Luckily I get the answering machine. She is probably out of town. I say, 'Mum it's me, Daddy is lost, call when you get a chance, thanks, it's Shell.' As soon as I put it down I want to call back because I am agonizing over the phrase 'Daddy is lost'; 'missing' would have been better, 'lost' sounds so foolish, as though I am confirming the policemen's notion that he is senile and wandering somewhere. Before I can pick up the phone to clarify the message I hear Robert's voice.

My brilliant cousin Robert is here to save the day. Robert has all the confidence that I lack; Robert, with his MBA from Georgetown University, his *magna cum laude* from Harvard, and his internship in London, makes me feel as though I've been napping for most of my life. My father is Robert's godfather but they have never been very close. A godparent, as Auntie B says, is supposed to lead his godchild to God. But my father has never been a very religious man and my mother only took us to church to appease the Carter clan and her own mother when she was alive. The prayers we said at night were made up by the three of us; a combination of the Our Father and phrases from poems or songs my mother may have liked at the time. She would let us add anything we wanted before we said the Amen. Robert had to rely on Auntie B and Uncle Paul for his religious education but both Simon and I know that it is part of a bravo performance rather than an expression of deep faith.

My brilliant cousin Robert has only ever been kind to me; he has always tried to help me yet everything he does and says irritates me more and more: the way he walks, talks, enters a room, always with the assurance that this background affords him. In the Carter clan the university you attended is one the markers of success, particularly amongst the cousins; those of us in the family who have studied abroad and not gone to the local university believe we have something that sets us apart from our cousins who studied at home. There is a feeling of superiority whether justified or not. Some of us feel this quietly, others cultivate this foreign edge in accents, lifestyles or dress, like Robert. He is so much like Uncle Paul it always amazes me: the booming voice, the successful businessman's laugh that seems to decide on how long a joke should last, the charming command taken in situations that demand a leader. I can just imagine Simon shrinking before him.

I hear Robert letting the policemen know that he has spoken to this one and that one – every name a high official to ensure that a proper search is conducted. There is a definite change in the tone of the discussion and even though Robert still irritates me I am happy to see the cocky policemen off balance. Whether they wanted to take my father's disappearance as serious or not, they now have no choice. Before returning to the living room I wait to hear the officers leave, promising to get back to us later in the day. A cell phone rings. It's Robert's. Auntie B calling, she wants to know everything and I can hear a slight sharpness in Robert's voice as he answers and repeats the same information again and again. As I walk into the living room I look at Simon; my brother seems deflated, exhausted and even sad.

As soon as Robert puts the phone in his pocket he jumps up to give me a strong embrace.

'How are you holding up, Shell?' he says, pulling me to sit next to him on the sofa facing Simon.

'I've had better days.' I am still staring at Simon while I speak to him.

'I took a drive around the neighbourhood to look for him, to see if I he was…'

But before Robert can finish, Simon shouts, 'He's not some bloody lost dog, Robert!'

Robert, typically, remains totally composed, says nothing but just looks at Simon as though my brother has lost his mind. Then Robert continues to speak in an overly calm manner, another way of correcting Simon's behaviour. 'I also passed in at the shop on the corner, they hadn't seen him and then I went as far as the tennis courts but he hasn't been there in months. Does he still play?'

'So now the entire neighbourhood knows that he is missing?' Simon says, still angry with Robert.

'Well, Si, correct me if I'm wrong but is it supposed to be a secret? I mean isn't the goal here to find Uncle Johnny?'

Before Simon can respond the phone rings. It's my mother. Auntie B must have found her. I hear Simon's voice change; the anger towards Robert has left and now exhaustion and quiet despair have set in.

'No, yes, yes, no, Robert is here, Uncle Paul is away… yes we think since Thursday but he may have come back in on Friday night, Shell found a cup and saucer by the bed… not a word. OK thanks, yes I will, they're fine, thanks Mom, hold on. Shell, Mom.'

Simon walks inside as he hands over the receiver. My mother's voice sounds far away; the connection is not very good; she is still in London visiting friends and her eldest sister, my Aunt Yvonne. I would like to sound angry and cold but I don't. I am almost forty years old and the sound of her voice can send me back decades; I wish she were here to solve it all for us, to bring my father home.

'Listen, Shell, don't panic, if, God forbid, something really terrible had happened we would know, we would feel it. Your father has done this before, or rather used to do this when you and Si were younger, go away for a day or so, to get away, take a break, but he'll come back. Did you call Mac?'

'No, I don't think he's still in touch with Mac.'

This name, Mac, is anathema in our family. When we were quite young, my father's liming partner was Mac, a distant cousin. My mother hated Mac for his crude manners, his terrible taste in clothes and women, but most of all for his drinking. I never liked Mac, neither as a child nor as an adult. He had a way of staring at you that made you feel as though you were standing naked before him. But that was not what I disliked most about him; what I hated was the persona my father took on when Mac was around. A fake-jovial, one-of-the-boys kind of mannerism and speech turned my father into Mac's lackey.

'Listen, Shell, I know this is hard to hear but your father has started spending a fair amount of time with Mac again.'

I remain silent.

'I've been in touch with Uncle Paul; he has seen your father and Mac together.'

I am still silent so she says, 'Are you still there Shell?'

'Yes, but I speak to Dad almost every night and I am here every Saturday morning. I don't see when he could be drinking with Mac?'

'Listen Shell, your father wouldn't want you to know. When you were young, I used to spend entire nights waiting for Mac to bring him home at dawn.'

These are not new stories. My mother has told them before but she refuses to stop bringing up her trials with my father in his drinking days as though this will wash away all of her own sins. Wasn't she the one who would boast at family gatherings that my father gave up drinking for her? I do not remember my father ever drinking in front of us, and how many long speeches have Simon and I had to endure from our father about drinking and driving. I want to ask my mother right now if she thinks all these old stories will make me forgive her. But I don't say a word. In fact I have been silent for so long that I hear her ask to speak to Simon.

From the easy way Simon speaks to her I realize that they talk more often than we do. I can also tell that Simon knows about Mac and this is something he has kept from me. Secrets, hiding things, surprises; I hate them all, I hate not knowing when everyone else in the family does. Does Maria know about my father? Does her snotty family know? The old familiar feelings return: jealousy, anger, being on the outside, outside of my mother's life, Simon's life and now my father's life, outside of this circle that knows my family secrets. Almost forty and I am still letting them tear me apart.

Simon seems to get courage from my mother; after he comes off the phone, Robert can no longer get under his skin. Simon is back in control; in command because my mother has told him exactly what to do. He calls Mac's house; this is another indication that Simon has been through this before. Mac isn't there his son says; in fact he's been gone since Friday morning. He hasn't heard from him but sometimes he goes up to the family beach house overlooking Maracas Bay. Simon asks whether Mac was alone or with our father John Carter. But the son can't say. Robert thinks that we should drive up to the beach and see if we find the two men. He calls Auntie B to let her know what we are about to do and Simon calls Maria. I get my handbag and wait outside on the porch. But at the last minute I decide not to go.

'I'll wait here, just in case he calls, or in case the police want to get in touch with us.'

This is what I say but I really do not want any other image of my father but the one I see on Saturday mornings when he sits on the porch pretending not to wait for me. I have already imagined him drunk and dishevelled, slouched under some grass hut on the beach with Mac surrounded by empty rum and beer bottles, stinking of sweat and urine like two nasty vagrants. Simon tells me not to worry and Robert gives me a quick kiss on the cheek. When they leave I decide for some reason to call my mother again. This is an act of courage for me; no one can imagine how easy it is for her to wound me; the slightest inflection of her voice, any sign of disapproval or disappointment and I feel lost for weeks. We are strangers, my mother and I, always have been, even before she left. And I know that I will never truly be able to forgive her. But I do not say all of this when I call back.

'Simon and Robert just left.'

'They'll find him Shell, don't worry. When you and Simon were younger he would do this all the time.'

Again she insists but luckily says nothing more and neither do I even though we talk for almost an hour, until we get the call saying that they have found my father at Mac's house. While we wait for that call I tell my mother about the job at the bookstore and M. Singh's verbs that stay forever in the present tense. She tells me stories about her editors and how much she has to explain to them about her where she is from. After all these years she says, 'They still look at me like some strange, exotic fruit.' 'That's funny,' I say, 'Not funny ha ha, but funny strange.' So I tell her about my Rambutan theory, leaving out the part about her being a Rambutan herself. We talk, keeping each other company while we wait for that call about my father and I feel as though it's the first time I've spoken to my mother in years.

THE DOLPHIN'S SMILE

From the room upstairs, I can see Uncle Joey's boat coming towards our jetty, leaving, like the feathers of a giant rooster's tail, a fluffy white wake. *The Dolphin* is filled with guests dressed in black or white; these ghosts float over the green patch of sea we call the Savannah. Mr Black, our caretaker, has been going back and forth all morning, bringing them across to my grandfather Papa Sam's island. Our guests, still afraid of Papa Sam even though they buried him a long time ago, have now come to pay their respects to his dead son, Joseph Samuel Linton.

My Uncle Joey used to smile at everyone but he didn't have a lot of friends. He lived a lonely life, never had a wife and never shouted orders at us like my mother or Auntie Bee. Uncle Joey wouldn't have wanted a big funeral; he never liked to be around a lot of people and spent most of his time on his boats fishing in the Savannah. My mother Sisi, my Auntie Bee, Uncle Tony, my cousins Loulou and Rachel, my brother Robby, the men who took care of Uncle Joey's boats, Mr Black and me, that would have been enough people for my Uncle Joey. But Auntie Bee gave her brother a funeral Papa Sam would have been proud of; she invited the government minister and his minister friends who rented our house to the north of Papa Sam's bay, Old Man Lee's family who rented our house on the western side, other wealthy Chinese businessmen, their neat Chinese wives and the oldest of the old, weathered, leathered, French Creole families. She hired two caterers (one for the meal, one for the dessert), three barmen and lots of waiters and waitresses. The deck looks more like a wedding than a funeral with the white tents, the well-dressed guests and the white sleeves floating endless trays of hors d'oeuvres and champagne.

Pelicans are diving into the Savannah; it must be full of fish today. When I look down from the window, the water is unusually clear, a Tobago-green clear. A school of neon-green fish zigzag across the rocky, shadowy seabed. On days like this, you can see cars on the mainland, houses on the hill above Irish Bay and even Venezuela on the horizon. I woke up this morning in the room I used to share with my brother Robby when we spent weekends on Papa Sam's island and I prayed for rain. Not a light, fine rain but a heavy downpour, a sudden tropical storm that would last all day, drench the guests, the tents, the food and make the crossing to Papa Sam's island impossible.

I didn't see Rachel and Loulou come off the last boat trip but I hear them downstairs; their voices haven't changed. Rachel still has her sweet high lilt and everything Loulou says still sounds like an order. Their voices trail out of the house and now I can finally see my lovely first cousins on the deck. Rachel has cut off all her hair and looks even more like my Uncle Joey with her big, watery, green eyes and sunny brown skin. Loulou still resembles Uncle Tony's side of the family; she has their thick eyebrows and wavy, blue-black, shiny, ink hair. They are the same height (Loulou used to be much taller), both in long, narrow, black pants and white shirts, like magazine girls, made-up, pretty and thin. We haven't seen each other since my mother took Robby and me to Boston, seven years ago. They used to say I had Papa Sam's slanted Chinese eyes and my Granny Nina's light, fine hair but now I'm just fat and plain-looking because my mother still forces me to eat everything on my plate and dress like some hippie kid in the cheap, crappy clothes she buys at flea markets outside Boston. She won't even let me cut my hair like the other girls in my high school because her boyfriend, Richard the Vegetarian, whom Robby and I call Veggie Dick, believes 'young ladies should look like young ladies'.

My mother laughs, then whispers something to Loulou and Rachel. I'm sure the joke is about me; she's telling them to bring me downstairs to talk to the guests. She knows I hate having all these intruders on our island.

Papa Sam's horseshoe bay, his three houses, the sea, the trees on the hill and Mr Black's cottage all look the same but everything has changed. How is it that Loulou and Rachel can stay downstairs with those hypocrites? Why don't they rush upstairs to me and ask why Robby won't come back to Papa Sam's island even though he hates that city of grey houses and grey people? Why don't they want to sit across the bed, the way we used to when they sent us upstairs to take a nap? Together, we could remember the day we saw that beautiful raft in the water near the Lee's side of the bay, the day we broke all the rules and swam across.

'I preferred it when it was yellow,' Rachel said. 'That pink is too pink and now it makes the sea look darker, like thick, black soup.'

My brother Robby never liked to agree with anything Rachel said because in those days he could barely stand to look at her; the more Robby looked, the more he had to push all of Rachel's prettiness away from him.

We kept talking about the colour of the house and I honestly can't remember who suggested that we swim across the bay to have a closer look. It could have been Robby's idea, it could even have been mine; I'm still not sure. It didn't matter; we decided to do it even though we all knew it was against the rules. They told us we could swim near our side of the bay but not beyond an imaginary line across the water that Auntie Bee and Uncle Joey had drawn for us. According to Auntie Bee, these people were paying a lot for their privacy, so we were to leave them alone.

'Get away from the window!' said Loulou, dragging Rachel back onto the bed, but she pulled her so hard that Rachel's foot hit and broke a glass under Auntie Bee and Uncle Tony's bed.

'See what you made me do.' Rachel had tears in her eyes.

'Why do you have to be so rough?' Robby was standing in front of Loulou. 'Now we're going to have to stay up here for the rest of the day.'

'Sisi can go downstairs and get the dustpan so we can clean it up.' Loulou sounded exactly like Auntie Bee.

Even though I tried to protest, I knew it was useless. Three against one, I never won. They told me to go to Auntie Bee, say we had spilled some powder on the floor and come right back up with the dustpan and the hand broom. The stairs creaked even though I tried my best not to make a sound. Everything was quiet and calm downstairs except for the fat raindrops hitting the water and the sound of thunder coming from the mainland. Auntie Bee was lying on a deckchair with a towel wrapped around her waist, her eyes were closed and the rain was falling on her face. I heard muffled voices coming from the water where Uncle Joey and Uncle Tony were swimming. On the table next to Auntie Bee was Uncle Tony's half-empty bottle of red rum and the tray of soggy cheese sandwiches we had had for lunch. Soaking white paper napkins were scattered all over the deck.

I tiptoed toward the cupboard and managed to pull out both the dustpan and hand broom without making a sound. As I turned to go back up the stairs, laughter from the water woke Auntie Bee.

'Sisi?"

I froze.

'What broke?

'Nothing, Auntie Bee, just some powder spilled…' but before I could finish I started to cry.

'Come here, Sisi,' Auntie Bee held out her arms. 'You know you can't tell a fib to your Auntie Bee.'

I dropped the broom and dustpan and went to her; she made room for me on the deckchair, wrapped her soft, fleshy arm around me, then kissed my forehead over and over again. I still know that smell of rum, rain and sea.

More laughter from downstairs; I even hear my mother's girlish, hiccupy giggle. Veggie Dick is in our poky, rent-controlled Cambridge apartment, babysitting Robby, so she is free to flirt with all her old boyfriends. This is my first funeral. Granny Nina and Papa Sam died in the same year, but we were too young to go to their funerals. Robby remembers that time when our father was still around. I don't. I don't even remember playing games with our father but Robby swears we did. Robby knows our father's voice; he says it sounds like rough seas or like waves crashing onto the rocks. In the framed picture we have of him, I only see a stranger with no voice; a tall, thin man with a beard and a Panama hat, hugging my mother on an empty beach.

I miss my brother. Only Robby can explain why they are all acting as though Uncle Joey is in the next room, waiting to come and make a speech thanking everyone for coming to his funeral. Robby would be able to tell me why Loulou and Rachel (our favourite cousins) are not upstairs, looking down at all these strange, sweating, powdery faces on our deck.

If I had told Auntie Bee the truth about that day, that we wanted to swim across to the Lee's side, maybe Robby would be up here in the room with me. But then I would have betrayed my brother and cousins. I kept my secret. Robby says everyone has secrets and some of them should stay under the water forever.

The day Uncle Joey took Robby for a ride in his boat without the rest of us was supposed to be a secret. Uncle Joey warned Robby that if he said anything Loulou, Rachel and I would get jealous, but Robby still told me. He said that Uncle Joey even let him steer and throttle, making huge, white rooster tails. That was the day he saw the dolphins diving in and out of the sea, so close to the side of the boat he touched their wet rubbery skin. Uncle Joey took Robby into all the different bays: China Man's Bay, Yankee Bay, Irish Bay, all the way to Shepherd's Bay with the church that grows out of the black rocks so the islanders can have Mass on a Sunday morning without going over to the mainland. Robby saw the small caves on Centipede Island where Papa Sam would threaten to leave Uncle Joey when he was a boy. Robby didn't like the caves but he loved it when they passed Eros, the last of the islands, where the parrots lived. Beyond Eros was the line of the horizon. As they headed out to the open sea, the water became choppier, the waves higher, but Robby didn't mind. He loved the wide, open space connecting them to every other ocean in the world. Before they reached the Boca, heading towards Tobago, they turned back.

Seeing that beautiful raft in the water made us break the first law of Papa Sam's bay – to stay on our side. Mr Lee's grandchildren used to come to the island on the last Sunday of every month. The last weekend of the month, our mother didn't come with us but sent us down so she could 'take a break and relax'. Mr Lee's grandchildren always had shiny, new toys that glistened in the dark, bush-green water. While they swam or jumped off their deck, they hardly made a sound. Their side of the bay was always very quiet, unlike ours. We hated these 'little darlings' that Auntie Bee and Uncle Joey admired.

Auntie Bee had fallen asleep with her arms still wrapped around me. I must have dozed off as well because the sun had come back out and my cheeks were burning. Carefully unwrapping myself, I went inside and crept past Uncle Joey who had dozed off looking at a cricket match on TV. The door to the guestroom was half-open; Uncle Tony lay sprawled on his back, still in his swimming trunks. When I walked into the room upstairs, Rachel, Loulou and Robby were sitting across the bed, facing the window. They had seen Mr Lee's grandchildren pack away their big, yellow raft with its orange bumpers and green paddles in the storeroom, then go inside their giant-conch-shell-coloured house to take their afternoon nap like four perfect little Chinese dumplings.

'Why did you take so long to come back up? We had to clean up the mess with toilet paper,' snapped Robby.

Then they asked their favourite spy where everyone was because they were ready to swim across. After my report, we decided to make our move. Instead of crossing the bay from the deck, we swam from the jetty, around Uncle Joey's boat. The crossing would take more time but there would be less chance of anyone hearing us. Loulou usually swam the fastest but that day

Robby did a perfect crawl across the bay while the rest of us doggy-paddled. Sometimes he dived in and out of the water like a dolphin, making a half-moon, then plunging into the sea again.

I know why they won't come upstairs; they've heard about my visits to psychologists, specialists and whateverists, people who try to help me with problems they create. My mother and Veggie Dick believe Robby and I need 'to explore our feelings of anger and resentment'. They're afraid we'll end up like those crazy American children who play real-life video games shooting class bullies, teachers and cheerleaders. According to my mother, therapy helped her 'to deal with her childhood'. So both Robby and I know all this therapy she claims is for us is really for her. Rachel and Loulou must know about it, that's why they're staying away from me. They're afraid that their 'favourite little cousin' will suddenly attack them with the Swiss Army knife she has tucked into the boxer shorts she wears under her ugly, black and white, paisley-patterned dress.

Robby sat on the Lee's deck, waiting for us.
'Hurry up, slow coach!' He quickly covered his mouth, re-membering he shouldn't shout. 'They're still napping upstairs.'
I was the last to climb onto the Lee's new wooden deck. We all went to the side of the house. There was a very narrow path between the dry, rocky hillside and the ground floor. We had been across once before, when Uncle Joey and Mr Black went across to check a leaking water tank at the back of the house and only Mr Lee's thin, quiet son had been there.
Robby and Loulou tried to lift me high enough to peep into the storeroom through the porthole window. It was dark but I was sure I saw something that looked like a raft.
'If the door isn't locked, we can borrow the raft for a little while,' Loulou said.
Then it suddenly began to get dark again; grey clouds, like

thick smoke, covered the blue sky. The sea looked black and deep.
Soon everything, the hills on the mainland, the tugboats, the
yachts, all would disappear behind a giant white sheet of rain.

'We should go back now.' Rachel looked as though she was
about to burst before the clouds. 'What if when it starts to rain the
water gets too rough and Sisi can't make it back to our side?'

'Sisi isn't afraid to swim across, you are.'

'Shut up, Robby.' Rachel turned around and walked towards
the water. I could already hear her spinning tales in her head to tell
Auntie Bee and Uncle Joey.

'Come back here and wait for us.' Loulou grabbed her by the
arm. Rachel stooped down and began to cry.

After that, it all starts to get a little fuzzy in my mind. Loulou
pulled Rachel towards the water and I followed. No one realized
that Robby hadn't jumped off the deck with us. It was only when
we got to our side of the bay that Loulou asked, 'Where's Robby?'

Before we could answer, Uncle Joey was standing in front of
us. I avoided even a glimpse of his face. Over and over again he
asked, 'Why did you go to the other side of the bay?' Even after
Loulou kept saying she was sorry and Rachel kept crying, Uncle
Joey acted as though he hadn't heard a word. Then suddenly he
realized Robby wasn't with us.

'We think he's still on the other side,' Loulou said softly.

When we went to Boston with my mother, Robby and I made
a pact that we would never betray each other. I never told my
mother or Veggie Dick when Robby tried to run away but only got
to Au Bon Pain in Harvard Square, or when he bought *Playboy* and
Penthouse from a boy at school, or when he stole chocolates from the
CVS, or even when he cut an Irish boy with his penknife on our way
home from Fenway Park because the boy called him a nasty island-
nigger boy. But that day 'down the islands', Loulou, Rachel and I
said it was Robby's idea to swim across the bay for the raft.

Uncle Joey said nothing; he just turned around to face Mr
Lee's deck. Old Man Lee was standing close to the water smoking
a cigarette, glaring at us from his side of the bay. His Hawaiian
shirt, always unbuttoned, exposed a huge balloon belly ready to

explode. His swimming trunks fell just below his hips. From the distance he looked exactly like Papa Sam. Mr Lee tossed his cigarette into the sea and continued to stare at us.

How can I describe my Uncle Joey's face right then? He looked like Robby just after my mother gave him a good cut-tail; he looked like Rachel after she saw a fat, black millipede on her pillow; he looked like Loulou after Auntie Bee slapped her across her face for being fresh. My brave Uncle Joey had left the deck and in his place stood a scared little boy.

Robby and I were afraid of different things. Robby hates the sounds he hears in the dark: the whispers, the cries, the moans, the whimpers and the gasps. I am afraid of the ghosts I see that seem to follow me everywhere I go. My brother's smile is like a dolphin's; it's always there, even when he is sad, you can still see it, but when he is afraid, the corners of that wide smile quivers.

When the little boy left and Uncle Joey was back, he sent Loulou and Rachel upstairs but told me to stay with him.

'Where is your brother?' he asked.

(Am I my brother's keeper? Or my mother's for that matter? Who can keep anyone?)

'I don't know, Uncle,' I said.

'Your mother and I were very close when we were small, just like you and Robby. I took care of her and she took care of me. We protected each other. But your grandfather was strong, just like Mr Lee, so you see, Sisi, we have to find Robby first.'

I know now that my Uncle was not trying to scare me or make me think that Mr Lee was about to cut Robby into pieces like a dolphin and use him for bait to catch sharks at the mouth of the Gulf. But what Uncle Joey didn't know was that I was more afraid of never seeing that dolphin smile again than I was of Old Man Lee.

Uncle Joey stared at the murky water as if he expected Robby to emerge from the bottom. After a heavy rain, the sea was always dirty, full of twigs, old paper, dead yellow or brown leaves and a white froth we called sea vomit. I glanced across the bay just in time to see Mr Lee go into the house.

'Maybe he went around the back by the hill, climbed over the fence and…'

Before I could finish, Uncle Joey had already started to make his way to the caretaker's cottage. It was as though he had finally woken up from a bad dream. Sometimes that waking up can take minutes or sometimes it can take years. My mother made Robby see Dr Epstein because he kept dreaming about Papa Sam, Mr Lee, my mother and me. Long after Robby and I moved to Boston to live with Veggie Dick, Robby still dreamt the dreams he had packed in his suitcase when he left Papa Sam's island.

Uncle Joey, Mr Black and I found Robby on the hill, at the back of Mr Black's cottage, with his hands wrapped around his body, rocking back and forth and muttering something we could not understand.

She is coming up the stairs; the prayers have begun. Uncle Joey's ashes will soon be tossed into the sea. My back faces her; I am looking at Mr Lee's deck across the bay. Old Man Lee died a few years ago, but I can still see him, his shorts low on his waist, his shirt open, with smoke coming out of his nose like a dragon.

'Come on, Sisi,' my mother says. 'Everyone is there.'

'Not Robby,' I say without even turning around.

There is a sigh, a general I-give-up sound and she leaves me again. For all my mother's evolutions and revolutions, she is still obeying the wishes of her father, Papa Sam, even though she says she is here for her brother. So soon, I will go downstairs, say hello to all the guests, kiss my slutty-looking cousins, smile at my drunk Uncle and recognize the sweet smell of gin and perfume on my Auntie Bee's dress.

After my Uncle Joey and I brought Robby back, his muttering stopped and then the yelling, screaming and howling began. We blamed each other, we cried and we begged but Robby never said a word. They threatened to leave us on Chacachacare Island (the old lepers' colony) or on Carrera (the prisoner island) if we ever went across to the other side of the bay again.

Later that night, when Robby and I were alone in our room overlooking the bay, he sat on the floor and started to rock back and forth again.

'Tell me about the time you saw the dolphins with Uncle Joey,' I said to him in the darkness.

'I never saw any dolphins, it was just a lie.'

'Yes you did, Robby. Uncle Joey said you did.'

'Uncle Joey is a liar.'

'That's not true, you're the big, fat liar,' I said, trying my best not to cry.

'Shut up! You don't know, you'll see, you don't know anything.' Robby got up from the bed and walked towards the window but he bumped into the chair.

'Ouch!' He tried to muffle a whimper.

'I saw Mr Lee,' he whispered. 'He was kissing his granddaughter down there.'

'Down where?'

'Down there, on her bud. Her dress was pulled up and she was just staring up at the ceiling and his head was on her bud.'

'Did Mr Lee see you?'

'I think so, but I don't care anymore.'

'What if he tries to come over for you or for us?'

'He won't come,' Robby said then got into his bed, pulled the covers over his head and turned to face the wall.

Not long after our talk, Robby started to get the dreams, but the dreams, like the story about Mr Lee, changed all the time; sometimes he saw Papa Sam or Uncle Joey and not Mr Lee, sometimes he saw our mother as the one being kissed, other times he saw me and once Robby even saw himself being kissed by Uncle Joey.

I am standing next to my mother on the deck but we are not alone: Papa Sam, Uncle Joey and Granny Nina are there too. My grandmother, who seldom spoke when she was alive, whispers to me (in between prayers) that the cancer that killed Uncle Joey was the same cancer that killed his father, Papa Sam; that Uncle Joey died on his boat (*In the name of the Father*), that he was not alone (*the Son*), that he was showing another little boy (*and the Holy Spirit*) like Robby the dolphins (*Amen*).

KILLING MOONS

It was Easter Sunday, Mama's birthday. The yard was still, so quiet you could hear the tide coming in. There was no sea breeze, not a cloud in the sky, only a bright, blue sea above my head. All my brothers and sisters were at the beach, helping the fishermen pull in the nets. If the catch was big, the fishermen would reward us with slippery, silver Jacks. Nana, Mama's sister, was sitting on our front steps shelling pigeon peas; she broke their spines and dropped the little green pebbles in a coal pot. The shells fell on yesterday's *Guardian*. Nana did this every morning when pigeon peas were in season, so we could eat rice and peas, fried fish and, if we were lucky, a piece of fried plantain for lunch.

The midday sun made the hot, sandy earth sting my bare knees. I had been kneeling in the yard for an hour but that was my punishment. Nana would never let me stand. Kneeling, she said, would remind me that I was before God. On Judgment Day I would have to answer for all my sins.

'You think I'm a mind reader or what?' Nana suddenly said, looking up from her coal pot and from the trance she had been in for what felt like a year. She wiped the sweat off her forehead but, in a second, little silver balls lined her temple again. She wanted to know how it all happened; she wanted me to tell her God's truth.

I never looked at Nana eye to eye; in our yard, that was a sign of rudeness. Instead, I focused on an army of red ants attacking clumps of burnt rice in the gutter.

'It was really Brother Samuel's idea,' I said.

Nana cleared her throat and spat into the gutter. 'Doh think yuh blamin' dis on yuh brother,' she said.

'No, Nana,' I said, 'I not blaming this on Brother Samuel. But two days before Mama's birthday, Brother Samuel pulled me to the back of the house and told me that this year we were going to give Mama the best birthday gift. He said that what we were going to give Mama melted on your tongue like coconut bake and butter, like ten sugar cakes from Mr Frank's parlour. Then Brother Samuel came so close to my face I could smell his sour breath: 'Duck meat,' he whispered. Now I knew that only one person in Cumana had ducks besides Mr Frank, and I knew Brother Samuel wouldn't steal from him, so it had to be Miss McShine. I told Brother Samuel that stealing was not a Christian thing, it wasn't even a neighbourly thing. But Brother Samuel said that Miss McShine couldn't even count the five teeth in her mouth, far less miss a duck or two. And he said that once everybody's belly was full and their eyes heavy with sleep, no one would even care about where the ducks came from.'

Nana looked up and smiled, not a nice smile but one we all knew in the yard. A wide pink-and-gold smile that showed off her gums and two gold teeth. Earlier that morning, Miss McShine had run into the yard shouting 'Rape' and 'Murder'. Brother Samuel, the minute he heard the cries, crawled from beneath the bed where we both slept and jumped out of the window. Nana and Mama woke up; the weight of them both sitting on the mattress pressed the bedsprings against my body. Miss McShine moaned, 'Hate, envy, jealousy, always follow me, from town to Toco, from Toco to Cumana. Is not my fault my father left me a little money or that I take after my half-Scottish mother.' We had heard about her mother's good hair and fair complexion since birth.

Nana and Mama drew the curtains and looked through the window. It wasn't really a window but a big, square hole that Mr Frank had promised to fill with louvres. I heard Miss McShine say that early that morning, before sunrise, ten big Negro men broke open her bedroom door. They asked her for her gold and her money. The biggest Negro man touched her in a place she would prefer not to mention. She gave them all she had, except for the money she had hidden in the outhouse. Each and every single one of those Negro men wiped their nasty sweat on her clean white sheets. Then they went into her yard. Peeping behind her lace curtains, she saw the tall muscular one, the same one who had interfered with her business, break fifteen of her ducks' necks with his bare hands and wipe the blood on his dirty, torn pants. Then they each grabbed a duck or two and left her home. All this because people were 'jealous her colour'.

After Miss McShine left our yard at sunrise, I cried quietly because Brother Samuel had left me alone. He knew Nana and Mama had ways of finding out the truth. For breakfast that morning Nana fried a bake for each of my brothers and sisters. With only one left, she looked at me and said, 'Where is Brother Samuel?' I looked down at my plate and muttered that I didn't know. Then Mama said, 'You two never more than a breath away from each other and you say you don't know.' My other brothers and sisters started to giggle.

Before that morning, I used to believe that Brother Samuel and I would always be together. But I remembered that Nana used to say that some men never drank from the same well twice, that some men said that too many dips dirtied the water. And Mama used to say that as soon as my breasts began to swell she would tie my cords so I wouldn't be able to have any children for these nasty men. I didn't want any children anyway and I didn't want any men in my yard. I prayed silently repeating, 'Please, God, don't let Brother Samuel be like one of those men.

The sun was so hot everything looked yellow and blurry.

'Look, child,' Nana said, 'I don't have time for yuh daydreaming. I giving yuh a chance to explain only because is Mama's birthday. But if you decide to be rude today, the only food you will taste is this!' She raised her hand.

Sometimes I couldn't figure out which one I hated more, Mama or Nana. Mama talked less than Nana, but Mama's punishments were just as hard. Today I wanted Nana to die first. Just then Mama stepped onto the porch, wearing her favourite pink-and-gold dress that she saved for weddings, baptisms and funerals. Papa raised his head out of the hammock and whistled, 'Girl, yuh lookin' too sweet.'

'Girl, Girl?' Mama said with a wide smile that showed her two gold front teeth, 'You see any girl here?' Then she giggled and covered her mouth.

Nana stood up to let Mama go down the steps. 'I hope you see many more,' Nana said. She wiped her mouth and gave Mama a quick peck on the cheek.

Although they were sisters, Mama and Nana looked nothing alike. First of all, Nana was twice Mama's size. Nana's skin reminded me of shiny aubergines. Her hair was like blue-black ink; it was long and wavy and smelt of coconut oil. Every morning Mama would plait Nana's hair so Mama's hands always smelt of coconut oil. When Mama was a little girl, people said that she would be able to run fast because her legs were long and skinny like mine. But Mama didn't like to run and she always said she never understood how people could run 'just for so', especially since she was always running behind so many children. Nana's skin would shine but Mama's skin was muddy, like dirt and milk. Her hair was gold, red and frizzy. In the morning, she would wet it, tie it and, for an hour or so, it would look as neat as Nana's but, as the day went on, it would change into a sunny ball of fur. I didn't look like Nana and I didn't look like Mama. They said I looked like my father. They said I was red like him, which meant that my skin was white and orange and my hair was like copper wire. I didn't know if they were right since I never saw him. If I had, no one told me who he was. I didn't care, especially since he didn't care what I looked like.

Mama had six children in all. Nana had none. Mama had many husbands but only my Brother Samuel and I had the same father. Brother Samuel was the eldest boy and I was the eldest girl and because of that we ruled the yard. All the other children had to obey our rules and I had to obey Brother Samuel's. But we all had to obey Mama and Nana. Papa came to the yard mostly on weekends. He ate, slept in a hammock between the coconut trees, then disappeared again by Sunday night. He wasn't anyone's Papa but that's what Mama told us we should call him. He couldn't tell us what to do; all Mama said was not to bother him.

Mama looked at me and shook her head. 'You and Brother Samuel will end up in the Toco police station one of these days.' Then she turned to Nana. 'I goin' into the village.'

'Take care,' Nana said. 'Today, today, you might make the shopkeeper leave that sour Chinee-of-a-wife.'

Mama giggled, then glided across the yard in her narrow dress with short, neat steps. Her hair glittered in the sunlight. She was going to see the shopkeeper, Mr Frank, who, everyone knew, loved Mama more than his own wife. The minute Mama disappeared, we could hear the dogs barking as she made her way down the street. Soon I could feel Nana's eyes on me again.

'Brother Samuel had a big stick, his soul stick, he called it. He showed me how to use it to kill ducks. I held it by the neck and practised hitting all the big rocks we passed on the way to Mr Frank's shop in the village. All Brother Samuel could do was talk about how sweet duck meat tasted. That morning, four stray dogs attacked us but Brother Samuel swung his soul stick like a cricket bat and hit the dogs for six. "Yuh see," Brother Samuel said, "this is a powerful piece of wood." When we told Mr Frank that the flour was to bake a cake for Mama's birthday, he gave us a bag of sugar free.'

Nana pushed herself up the steps; she stretched, rubbed her chest and belched. 'Gas,' she sighed. 'Listen to me. If Brother Samuel doh come home soon, I'll have to send you after those children and the fish.' Balancing the coal pot on her head, she took some heavy, slow, elephant steps into the house.

I was praying that Brother Samuel would stay away just long enough for me to go to the beach for fish. By now my knees were numb, my back hurt and my head pounded. Stealing was something Mama and Nana always told us we were never ever supposed to do. They said that poor people didn't have to steal, that only lazy good-for-nothing town people stole. Stealing was a sin, they said. One time Brother Samuel and I borrowed some Julie mangoes from the fat lady down the road. We told ourselves that as soon as our mango trees started to bear we would give some back to the fat lady. But the others saw us eating the fat lady's mangoes, and because we refused to share any with them, they went to Mama and Nana. That time Brother Samuel took the punishment. He had to kneel in the middle of the yard on a grater with a stone in either hand. He said that he never cried but I saw tears, not sweat, pouring down his face. Sometimes Nana would send us to the village to exchange figs for limes. Before we left, she would spit on the ground. We had to come home before it dried. So Brother Samuel would run ahead with the figs to look for Mr Simon, the caretaker on the Villain estate. The limes Mr Simon traded were Villain limes but Mr Simon said they were from his land. Everyone in the village knew Mr Simon had no land; he lived on Villain land, ate Villain food, stole and sold Villain limes. But we never teased Mr Simon because the Villain estate had everything. When I caught up with Brother Samuel, he would tighten my belt, fill my blouse with the limes, then we would run home faster than the spit could dry. One day red ants got into my dress. I ran into the yard screaming and scratching everywhere. Nana beat Brother Samuel because, she said, he was older and 'should know better'. Mama patted the stings with Witch Hazel and rubbed coconut oil all over my body. At night she fanned me and blew on the stings to cool them down and to help me fall asleep.

When Nana came back outside, I said, 'I told Brother Samuel that everyone would know we killed Miss McShine's ducks. But he said that you and Mama didn't care about that old witch because she was always shaming you and Mama.'

Suddenly Nana looked up.

'Brother Samuel said that Miss McShine told lies about Mama all over Cumana. Brother Samuel said that Miss McShine said that Mama took young girls into the yard and killed the babies in their bellies with hot hangers. And he told me that Miss McShine said that you didn't have any children because you didn't like men.'

'That old bitch,' Nana mumbled.

'Ah just repeating what Brother Samuel told me. He said that the only reason Miss McShine said all of that was because Mr. Frank preferred Mama and not her.'

Nana chuckled and then tried to look serious again. 'Go and bring the bag of rice by the sink.'

My legs felt heavy and wobbly but I was happy to get up. In the kitchen I put my mouth to the tap and drank and drank. Then I grabbed the bag of rice and tried not to spill a grain.

'Doh think yuh finish,' Nana said, taking the rice. 'Sit here.'

For some reason Nana was in a better mood, maybe because she liked what Brother Samuel had said about Miss McShine. Then again, with Nana you could never tell when she was about to hug you or hit you.

'Brother Samuel said that we would need bait for the ducks. So yesterday morning we went to the beach and begged the fishermen for bait before they took their boats out. The old one, Mr Kenny, gave us some shark meat.'

'Yuh said thanks?'

'Yes, Nana. Then Brother Samuel and I cooked the shark head and guts on the beach. Brother Samuel ate the head and I ate the eyes. We hid the rest in an old milk tin and buried it under the almond leaves at the back of the yard.

'When Brother Samuel woke me early this morning, it was still dark enough to see the cane burning across the sea. He took me to the outhouse and held my hand while I peed because it was so dark I thought I would fall into the pit. I waited outside the outhouse while Brother Samuel went to find the shark and his soul stick. The fish smelt really rotten and stank. I told Brother Samuel that if I was a duck I surely wouldn't eat it. But he said that ducks couldn't tell the difference between fresh fish and stale fish. He said that ducks ate anything. Then Brother Samuel and I ran our hands along the fence looking for the big hole Miss McShine had covered with a piece of galvanize. The hole was small but it was big enough for Brother Samuel to push me through. He giggled and said, "Yuh might be skinny but remember yuh strong as an ox." With one big push, I was on the other side.

'Brother Samuel told me that ducks never sleep; all the ducks were in Miss McShine's yard, their bodies shining like full moons that had fallen to the ground. "Hit them right between the ears, Suni," Brother Samuel said, poking his head through the hole in the fence. "Just like we practised."

'I scattered pieces of shark on the ground but the ducks didn't move. Then I realized they were behind a wire fence. "Brother Samuel, Brother Samuel," I whispered. "Shhh, Suni," he said. 'Just hit them between the ears, remember you strong as an ox.' I was a little scared but I thought that if I gave Mama a nice birthday gift she wouldn't ever punish me again. So I crawled into the wire fence towards the sleeping ducks. Then I raised the soul stick high above my head before I let the first blow fall. I hit as many ducks as I could, as strong as an ox. The ones that didn't die right away I beat on the neck until the body was still. It was just like killing moons and Brother Samuel's stick was full of magic.

'Ten times, Brother Samuel said, he called my name, but I didn't hear him. Then all of a sudden I stopped beating the last duck's neck. I looked around and counted seven dead ducks. I dragged them two at a time to the hole in the fence. Brother Samuel counted each one as he pulled them through to the other side. One, two, three… until he got to the seventh, then he said, "Oh God, Suni, yuh kill the whole flock."

'"No, Brother," I said, "I only killed seven." Brother Samuel began to moan, "Is now we going to jail, I said one duck, maybe two, but not seven." He pulled me through the hole. Then we piled the ducks onto a wheelbarrow. Brother Samuel said that we had to get rid of the ducks before the Toco police came.

'We wheeled the ducks as far as the bridge. Before we went any further, we looked to see if the road to Balandra Beach was empty. "This is the mouth of the river," Brother Samuel said. "The sea will swallow the ducks and pass them out in Venezuela." So that was what we did; we fed the seven ducks to the river before the sun came up this morning.'

Nana looked up and smiled. 'Between you and Miss McShine, the devil must be smiling this morning.' Then she stood up, looking like a big, black giant before me and said, 'Go and bring two buckets of water up to the house. Mama must be comin' home; I hearin' the dogs.'

That afternoon we brought the long table and two benches into the yard. My job was to sprinkle water on the ground to keep the dust down. All my brothers and sisters were at the table except Brother Samuel. Nana made a big pot of *pelau* with pigeon peas, rice and chicken. She also fried the big redfish Mr Frank gave Mama. Nana invited Mr Simon, the fat lady and her four daughters. Nana even invited Miss McShine, who told the story about the Negro men all over again, only this time she said they all touched her in unmentionable places. Nana and Mama just smiled.

I felt Brother Samuel's cool, early morning skin as he sneaked under the bed before the sun came up the next morning. He told me that he had followed the ducks all the way to Port-of-Spain and when he last saw them they were floating on their bellies like seven full moons on their way to Venezuela.

FOUR TAXIS FACING NORTH

From the fourth floor of the small balcony of the Pelican Hotel, I could see men bringing horses to the Savannah. Soon the sun would come up and all the shadows, spirits, and shades would disappear like the darkness, and the giant samaan and poui trees would fill out and become bodies again in the early morning light. In ten years this hotel would be owned by a huge oil company and there would be no more horses or horse track in the middle of the Savannah; they would cut down almost all of the samaan and poui trees. This very hotel would be gutted; the pool area filled for a car park; a traffic light placed at the edge of the grand semi-circular entrance so that the oil-company people could stop their cars and take a lunchtime jog around what they had left of the Savannah. To them the Savannah was just another piece of property; it was no Central Park for sure, but to us it was more than a huge, grassy roundabout in the middle of an island-city, to us it was like a heart; the roads from the Savannah ran like veins into that city of Port-of-Spain; from the Savannah you could get to any part of the city. It was our Mecca, our Jerusalem, with the power to renew and restore faith in the island-city. But to them it was just more oil-company real estate. So to pave half of it and butcher three hundred trees was not a sin; to get rid of the coconut carts, the oyster stalls, the boiled-corn vendors, the vagrants, the horses, the cricket pitch, the football fields, the snow-cone carts and the children, espe-cially the children who flew kites in the middle of the Savannah during kite season on a Sunday afternoon, was all part of the grand plan to clean up the island-city.

I know all of this, dear reader, because shades have a gift and I am a shade, but as the old men say, a gift may be a blessing but it can also be a curse. We are not born shades but shades are what we become when we move from one world into the other. Before I became a shade, when I was still a part of this family, I met a lady who was really a shade and whom I would come to call Virginia. It was outside a church in Bristol; she knew that soon I too would become a shade and so she wanted me to meet her in the first life so I would recognize her in the second. But I will explain it all to you, just give me a chance and some of your precious time, and trust me time means nothing in the second life, but it is priceless in the first; I know that now, so give me a little time, enough to hear a shade's short tale.

Last Night

Last night, in the hotel, I waited until the family, my old family, had fallen asleep before I began my flight through the night, my night flight; I saw the mother and father kiss their two children, a girl and a boy, walk softly through an adjoining door into their smaller bedroom and get into their oversized plump bed. That bed was made for angels; the sheets were clean, white and fresh, the pillows were so plump it was like resting your head on clouds; that bed held a promise of the sweetest sleep, but most nights the mother and father were haunted by shadows in their dreams. But tonight they were lucky, so sleep came quickly.

Flying at Night

Flying at night is easier than you may think; it has very little to do with your body strength and everything to do with your sight.

Every room on the eastern side of the Pelican Hotel overlooking the Savannah has a balcony with four white iron chairs and an iron table. The table and chairs have pretty filigree patterns of flowers and leaves joined together in a silly dance; these chairs provide a sturdy platform for my ascent into the night. Most times I fly, but once or twice I land on top of a maxi taxi or a private car and let the vehicle take me into one of the towns around the Savannah. There are grand buildings around the Savannah, places they teach you about in primary school; once or twice I have gone into the Museum, the Church, the Old Castle and the Tudor Residence. One night (a night I will tell you about later one) I even went into the Zoo, but what I saw there made me so distressed I could barely fly back to the Pelican because it is impossible to fly and cry. The level of concentration necessary for flight, especially at night, does not allow for any other thoughts but that of flying, particularly for novices like me.

The Town of the Gates

Around the Savannah, like concentric circles, there are many towns. In the first circle there is a town with some of the largest castle-houses on the island. The houses there are so tall they sometimes disappear into the clouds; the walls often touch the sky, so the only way to enter these castles is by sky or by land when the enormous iron gates open. Let me stop to describe the gates, dear reader, because they are amazing, covered in gold and silver and decorated with rubies, sapphires, emeralds and diamonds. Some gates have patterns of half moons and stars, others of musical notes that dance, some with crosses or palm trees, others with hibiscus and roses. The entrance into the castle-house must be done quickly, either as soon as the gate opens or by a high flying jump. But what is inside will also make you jump, I mean surprise you, maybe even scare you, for the people who live inside hide themselves well in the day but not at night. In the day they just look like regular home-castle owners in their black Benzes or fat black BMW Jeeps, but enter the house at night and it is another story. (*Note to reader*: Let me pause here because I want to let you know that what you are about to read is the truth, I have seen it with my own two shade-gifted eyes so you must trust me and more importantly believe me, know that I would never lie to you because in the second world we have little use for lies.) The castle owners, who just look like rich people in the day, become something else at night; they change, transform, metamorphose or whatever word you like, but just know that they do not look the same – they become jellyfish, yes jellyfish, fat, plump, rubbery and translucent, like the colour of a pale flesh-coloured panty hose; you can see their veins and their brains running through their bodies like drains: brains, veins, drains. The castle-houses have many rooms with gigantic golden beds that can hold a hundred people at once but at night the jellyfish sleep in their pools filled with emerald and turquoise tiles that make patterns of dolphins jumping in and out of waves. Hanging from the sky-high ceilings (because the pools are in the middle of the house and covered with glass ceilings) there are bottles full of tiny stars whose sparkling lights touch the water of the pool and then bounce off like gold and silver glitter. This is where they sleep, the jellyfish, the medusas, floating on top, as still as dead fish, their long tendrils hanging like the frills of a beautiful dress; they form a thick, round mass together at one end of the enormous pool. And I am not afraid, they cannot sting me, they cannot poison me, I can touch them, swim underneath them, entangle their tendrils, make bows, make long plaits, they cannot harm me, they can only poison each other in their sleep, for I am a shade.

The Savannah Horses

Early in the mornings, just as the sun is coming up over the hills around the Savannah, from the hotel balcony where I sit and wait for the sun to rise, I can see the old Indian men and young black boys bring the horses from the Police Barracks; I see the tops of their heads, smooth, grey and shiny or black and puffy. The young boys will exercise the horses, making them gallop into the middle of the grassy plain all the way to the old private cemetery and back again. The old men will tell them where to go, when to stop, when to give the horses water.

If I could change into any animal it would be a horse, and I know which one; a beautiful, proud, brown mare that a beautiful, proud, brown lady rides, with gold dust sprinkled on the mare and on her hair, which she wears in a long, brown plait that falls to her tiny waist and is the same colour as the brown mare's tail; the two of them, the lady and the mare, look like a dream. I do not want to know her name, or even hear her voice, just to see her is enough; her back as straight as a pole, her light trot. I would be her horse in a second, happy to have her ride me all day.

The Gift

With the gift of shades to see ahead, a gift that could be a curse because some things should never be seen ahead of time, I knew that in years to come they would destroy the Savannah and put a huge car park where the horses used to train and the race track used to be. Soon after I met Virginia I got very sick and stayed in bed for what felt like a hundred years, but it was only a few months before I fell asleep and woke up in the land of shades. You wake up in the land of shades at night and at first all you hear are voices from the old world and the new. The noise is almost unbearable at first but eventually you learn to quiet them one by one. You also wake up with the gift, so I knew all too soon that the house where my old family lived would be burned down by the very people who built it. Razed to the ground, dear reader, razed. Instructed by their leader, they were told to take back what belonged to them, they were told that the island was divided into haves and have-nots, fortunate and unfortunate, lucky and un-lucky, businessmen and beggars, and so the leader spoke to them in the hot sun, standing in the tray of a Mazda truck in the middle of a football field with a river on one side and coco trees on the other. And their leader told them to let the daylight see change, not the night, since it was their right to do this, and the leader said, 'For too long our people have had to use the cover of night to fight for what is rightly ours,' and he said, 'Go and the let old owners see the new ones.' They should not be ashamed: 'Go and claim what is rightly yours.' So they went into the valleys, the vales and the towns with homes some the size of castles, others a little smaller, and they told the old owners to leave with only the clothes on their backs. And some tried to resist but not many because they faced an army armed with cutlasses, rocks, knives and guns. And the old owners saw their houses burn in the day, not the night, and smoke was everywhere from the land to the sky. And it was the dry season so the fires spread across the hills, the gardens, and the lawns like a sheet, like gossip.

The mother took her handbag, the girl a book, the boy his magic pen and the father gathered all his courage to lead the family through the sweaty, angry, laughing, cussing, swearing, jeering, booing mob that had taken his house, his land and all of his pride. In truth the mob had nothing against the family, they were not like some of the others who drove past in their big Jeeps and never saw people walking at the side of the road in the mud or waiting for transport in white rain. The father would stop and give them a drop, the mother would smile and wave, and the children were friendly enough. So they let them go before they took what they wanted and burned down the house. Others were not so lucky. Before they burned their homes, they looted and gutted the houses, they made the living room a toilet, they kicked the fathers, sexed the mothers, and made the children watch even though they tried very hard to cover their eyes and their ears with their tiny hands.

But you didn't need a shade's gift to see that the have-nots would want to become the haves, you didn't need a shade's gift to see it. There were signs planted all along the way but no one wanted to read them, so it was only a matter of time, dear reader, precious time.

The Town of the Gutters

Just beyond the Town of the Gates and the bejewelled walls of the medusas and the emerald pools, in a second circle around the Savannah, there is another town, known to us all, and by us I mean the shades, as the Town of the Gutters. I never stay very long here because of the thick smells that rise from gutters, which are wide and swampy, filled with old blackened food, napkins, newspapers, dog shit, human shit (excuse me, dear reader, but by now, I am sure that these words are not as foul to you as they still are to Virginia, but shit is what we find in the gutters, so allow me a few shits here and there and possibly only one fuck – there), beer, rum, urine, lottery tickets, white spit, light-green phlegm, brown leaves, black mud, the pink arm of a doll, KFC boxes, a black doll's natty head, chicken guts and two cats' legs. The inhabitants of the town are nightwalkers; they do not sleep at night so it's hard to get around; they roam the sidewalks, they step into the gutters that are so wide they cover what is left of the road and the pavement, and in some areas the swampy gutters are so deep that the people need a boat to get from one side of the road to the other. The neon lights flash on the faces of old, grey, greasy-haired gamblers, matted natty-hair beggars, junkies, druggies and the juicy red-lipped ladies of the night. I usually fly very high to avoid the horrible smell, and once or twice I have almost fainted from the rotting-dog smell that seeps into the bodies of those street people and covers their skin like a cloth so they wear the smell and carry it with them everywhere they go. From way up in the sky they look like cockroaches, giant cockroaches bigger than rats or even cats, crawling all over one another, making a thick carpet that moves slowly in that gutter soup. I fly over the town faster than those flashing pink and red neon lights that line all the streets of that stinking Gutter Town.

The Mixing of the Waters

After their houses had been burned flat – *plat* to the ground, the haves who had now lost their homes had to walk to the nearest family or friend or sometimes even to the next hotel to find a place to sleep and rest their weary feet. The family, my old family, walked in silence, tears streaming down their faces but they did not say what they wanted to shout. And the towns were a bigger mess because suddenly in the middle of the dry season it began to rain, and the rains made all the pool water from the Town of the Gates flow into the Town of the Gutters, and so gutters mixed with pools and no one could really tell them apart, jellyfish and cockroaches in the same thick green pond. The family tried hard to wade through the waters as they got to the towns around the Savannah after they had walked over the Sans Souci hill. Their bodies moved slowly as though they carried house, fridge, stove, TV, DVD, SUV, ATV, and more on their backs. But they had no real load except for the memory of a home and of the child, their first born, they had left behind, burning flat-*plat* to the ground.

Time to Meet Virginia

When I fly, I do not always fly solo. Often I am not alone. The lady I first saw outside the church in Bristol helps me find my way. Her name is Virginia, like the state in America, she says, but her accent is not American, not Caribbean, not English, not French, not Italian or Cuban but a mix of all these. Her parents travelled a lot when she was a child and they loved driving through America, and so she could easily have been called Georgia, Florida or even Pennsylvania. So she is happy enough with Virginia.

Virginia prefers to spend 'her days in the shade' as she says, not in England or America but here with me on this island of fires and burning tyres and flooding waters. Virginia's shadow is with me in the day, and at night we move together alongside the other shades that circle the towns. Why Virginia chose to be my guide she will never say. Before we enter the world of shades our guides appear to us in the day; that way we recognize them when we wake up in the night with other shades. I was there outside the church in Bristol with the family because the mother loved churches and she wanted to light a candle for an old lady she had loved in any church that took her fancy as the family walked through Old Cities with great histories; the mother wanted to sit on a pew and remember the face, the voice and the old lady's gentle smile, but she also wanted to rest her weary feet for they often walked very long distances. The family followed her into every church: the father, the girl, the boy and me. There were two candles for the old lady in the Duomo in Florence, three in Notre Dame in Paris, one in a church in Madrid and now one in Bristol. Of all the churches the mother had seen she loved the one in Bristol the best. The tall narrow windows divided into red, blue, yellow and green blocks of light made the mother think of tiny dolls' houses. That was the church she would remember most; it wasn't grand or fancy but small and empty with the old grey-haired lady outside the church door offering the family a tour, and there was no one inside except us and that old lady, the one I would come to know as Virginia, soon to be a shade by my side, soon to be my guide.

Lessons from Virginia

Let me say this because it will happen to you, for we all become shades, eventually, so listen well, and it is this – when you are a shade and you are given the power of flight (and here you must trust me, you will fly) you will hear voices while in flight. At first they will sound like a million mutterers but then the mutters becomes louder and louder until you think your ears will burst, you cannot fly with all these voices, all this noise, just as you cannot cry and fly at the same time because you will lose your balance and fall. Shades are given the power to fly but they must first learn to quiet the voices. This is why we often need guides. Older shades who can teach us to remember what our own voice sounded like. Virginia taught me how to stop the voices, but it is a procedure too difficult to describe here and it takes a lot of time, which we (as shades) have but which you do not, so just trust me that the voices will stop in time, shade time.

Virginia taught me many more things: how to balance in flight, how to land, how to move in between other shades when there is traffic (because even here it is crowded, particularly at night) and she showed me the places to avoid to the north of the Savannah: the Zoo, the palace on the hill and the three churches, all with underground tunnels that take you to places where the things you see make you forget what your voice sounded like and where your gift to see ahead no longer works. The things you see in those places haunt you for a long, long time and even Virginia cannot make you forget the horrors you have seen. Virginia warned me about these places over and over again but I did not listen; it was early on in my travels, you see, and perhaps the freedom of the night flights made me neglect the fact that in every world there are rules. So I went into that tunnel on a flight without Virginia, the tunnel below the Zoo where the macaws screech and scrawl patterns in the air, and I remembered Virginia's lessons only when it was too late.

Virginia's Lessons About the Tunnels That I Should Have Listened To

1. 'In the tunnel you will want to turn back but once you enter you will never return to the same point of entry.' (I took that to mean there were other exits, but I learnt that it really meant that, even if I found the first point of entry, after the tunnel I would not be the same.)

2. 'Do not forgive them because they know exactly what they are doing; freedom does not come from the forgiveness but from the forgetting.' (This made little sense to me at the time but I know

now that the weight of pain and the images of such suffering make it hard to fly and shades must feel this lightness and master the act of forgetfulness in order to leave the ground.)

3. And *Notez Bien* (NB): the lessons in the tunnel only make sense after you have been there, so to really appreciate and understand the lesson you have to go, but once you go you wish you had listened to the first lesson which was not to go at all.

Virginia's Lessons That I Loved To Listen To

There were other lessons from Virginia I loved like the ones I received while sitting on a branch of an immortelle tree facing the hotel's 'Four Taxis Facing North' sign planted in the middle of the pavement. Virginia would start, 'Repeat after me, *chérie*' – then pause and say '*mer* means sea' – and I would say '*mer* means sea'; and '*mère* means mother' – 'and *mère* means mother'; '*méduse*, jellyfish' – '*méduse,* jellyfish'; 'they are all French' – 'they are all French'; '*nostos* is Greek, it means return, *salve* is Latin, it means salvation, *vol* is flight, *nuit*, night, *oscura* is shadow in Italian, *plat* is flat in French, *camin* is road in Italian.' And so it would go for hours and hours or even days at a time.

There were big English words as well: perfidious, perspicacity, pandemic, endemic. I listened well and repeated each one but I preferred the words in Italian, which soothed me and wandered through my thoughts like a cool stream. Virginia's lessons never ended until the day she left me at the 'Four Taxis Facing North' sign, and I will soon leave you to get on with your life, but please stay just a little longer for I promise we are nearly there. During my lessons with Virginia as my guide I did my lessons well and followed all the rules except one, the one I should have kept but didn't keep and still regret, and regret is no use to us shades.

The Forbidden City

The night flight I took into the Forbidden City (and I assure you it was a city and not a town) with all the underground tunnels that lead to the Zoo, the palace on the hill and the three churches, I took alone. My gift of sight was blackened from the moment I entered the tunnels. And from the moment I entered I wished I had listened to Virginia, but it was already too late. Still I felt as though she could see my every move.

I passed through the tunnels into wide gutters into a City of Rivers, rivers that were more like swamps; not like the swamps in the Town of the Gutters but real swamps with red mangroves with tall roots that looked like thin bent brown legs. I know by now you will trust me when I say that the swamp-rivers were wide, as wide as two American freeways with four lanes on either side, wider than the Seine, which I have seen with my own eyes, wider than the Thames, and I have seen that river too. The water was thickened with bush, grass, even seaweed; you could find a dead dog, a floating bloated carcass with its legs spread apart looking just like that poet said (one of Virginia's favourite poets who spoke about legs spread apart like a fat whore's), there were dead macaws, dead roosters, dead howler monkeys with eyes still wide open and mouths full of black flies buzzing and humming a crazy alphabet, like that other poet said. The air was so thick with smells and sounds that it slowed me down. I couldn't hear my own voice, I couldn't breathe, I should have turned back then and there – it was so hard to fly. But there are times, dear reader, when something pulls you to the forbidden, you feel it in your loins, your groin, it tickles you in a sweet way, your heart pulls and tugs and there is a moment of doubt in the desire but the sweetness pulls you, it makes you go on even though you know the sweetness cannot last, but by then it is too late.

As I came out of the tunnels I remembered all of Virginia's lessons: how to avoid touching the medusas' tentacles in the Town of the Gates, how high to fly in the Town of the Gutters or low in the Town of the Bats, to never enter the tunnels of the

Forbidden City, especially the tunnel that leads to the Zoo. But as I came out of one of the many tunnels and the City of Rivers I saw that sign and again I did not heed Virginia's lesson. I hope you will make the right choice when your time comes.

At the entrance to the Zoo there is a sign with a golden crown and a purple butterfly, it says 'The Zoo'. The name of the Zoo is 'The Zoo'. As plain as that, as though there is nothing fancy inside, as though the place has nothing to hide. At least that is the sign you see in the day but at night the sign becomes a movie screen that plays the same scene of an army of a hundred naked women with long hair and shaved, tickling, glistening pussies, all different yet all the same riding fat black bears or soft damp tigers, followed by a hundred young, naked boys with tiny marble testicles and two-inch dicks walking behind like little princes, each holding a pet panther with leashes made of plaited bamboo, gold and black leather. The Zoo, Virginia says, brings together water and fire, temptation and desire, all the paths that lead to Satan and Hosanna. But I enter, leaving the mother, the father, the boy and the girl in the hotel room asleep, at peace, at least for the moment before they start wandering through their dreams of falling off roof tops or running away from mobs or trapped in a house on fire.

If I were you, my dear reader, I would want to know what is the first thing you see as you enter the Zoo at night. But that is not the right question – imagine instead what you hear: the deep mournful moan of a mother howler monkey whose howl is deep enough to dig a grave for her half-eaten, dead monkey-child; imagine the echo of a lion's roar mixed with the shrieks of a thousand terrified macaws, a gigantic cayman's splash here, a snake's whisper there, a giggle here, a flutter there but then there is also what we do not hear. A shade hears the whimper of children, muffled screams, sighs of desire, a *frisson de jouissance* and *d'horreur* and the pleasure-filled braying of the Zookeeper at night. Half-man, half-beast, the upper half, man, the lower, beast, or sometimes the lower, man, the upper, beast, the lower half, goat, ram, mule or bull, the upper, a smiling Gringo, Mulatto, Chigro, Syrio, Indo or Afro. Flying over the Zookeeper's house, dear reader, you will see so many children all in an animal soup lying on the cold floor, shivering, shaking, slithering with snakes, bowing to bulls, mounted by mules, all taught to sing praises to the Zookeeper.

I could barely fly as I left that place knowing I should have listened to Virginia. The Zoo is no place for young shades, or even old ones for that matter. Before I could get to the exit I fell to the ground in front of the tigers because I was crying; it was the second time I had proved the lesson right – you cannot fly and cry. But I also remembered the lesson of powerlessness, because although shades can fly and have the gift of sight (except in the Forbidden City) shades have no real power. I could not help the children, or take them away from the Zookeeper; I left the boy on the wooden bench where his feet were tied with rubber and the little girl being tickled on the sofa; shades are space, air, wind, shadows and darkness full of freedom and of emptiness at the same time.

I managed to pull myself up and find another exit and who did I see but Virginia waiting at the gates of the Zoo. She knew the questions before I asked them.

Virginia's reply to question 1: 'The children come from the Town of the Gutters.'

Reply to question 2: 'The Zookeeper is an islander half medusa, half gutter, half monster-man, half man-monster.'

The Day of the Fires

Already a shade, aware of my gift, I knew they were coming. They came in the day, not the night, and the mother saw them coming up the wide quiet street lined with olive trees and immortelles, and the boy and girl were in the garden so she called to them and told them to put on their shoes and wait for her in the bedroom. The girl grabbed a book and the boy his magic pen. The mother went to the father who was already at the gate, the tall black gate at the end of a long driveway and the powerful scent of gardenias and jasmine filled the air. There was smoke too. In the distance the fires had started and soon a slate coloured cloud filled the sky, it moved fast like a huge sheet in the wind or a giant sail on the water, making the day night, casting shadows, stifling the smells of the gardenias and the jasmine, making them all shades for a moment. And more and more came in old rusty cars, or on bikes made from pieces of scrap, and the family grew more and more afraid, the frightened mother went into the bedroom with her children, the father's hands trembled at the gate, and the boy and girl looked out from the window upstairs in their parents' bedroom, terrified and excited at the same time. They all recognized the faces from the village, the vale and the hills of Sans Souci: the Indian man and his sons who sold pies and doubles at the corner, the Rasta who sold yams and cassavas, Mr White's gardener, Mrs Charles's housekeeper, the boys on the bikes, the Scotts' housekeeper's son, Hassan, but there were many more faces they didn't recognize, and they all held cutlasses, knives, guns, big sticks, and some of the women held large empty crocus bags or big black garbage bags soon to be filled with the treasures of the house before they burned it down. The mother ran inside to her children and the father stood at the gate, the once quiet street now filled with shouts, screams, jeers, laughter, threats, and cussing. He could smell the rum, the cheap scotch, the ganja, the sour sweat and the dirt. But the father didn't resist, he had no weapon, his dogs had been poisoned a week before (he should have seen this as a sign – my God they had been planning this for a while). He was afraid for himself, his wife and his children. The father didn't resist but they still beat him anyway.

The Walk Away

They beat the father, not badly because he didn't resist, a few kicks to the knee, a blow to the back, a butt to the head, a few shoves from the younger Muslimeen boys; they said a few nasty things to the mother but they never touched her, at least not her body but she was touched forever. The mother walked away from the burning house with her son, her daughter and her husband, knowing that as soon as they had taken or broken everything they had worked so hard for they would burn it down. A new madness had taken over the valleys, the vales, the cities and streets; the entire island. The rivers were yellow, the tap water was brown, the sea was red, the sky the colour of smoke, villages were at war, divided into tribes, neighbours became sudden enemies, there were rapes, murders, beatings, shootings, kidnappings, all at once, and still all the mother could think about was the sick child, her first born, whom she had carried for nine months, raised for fifteen years, and lost a year before in the very house they were burning down, the year I became a shade.

Black Gold

Well, dear reader, all that talk of the end, the apocalypse, the four horsemen, rain, floods, *tremblements de terres*, did not win out over the oil companies who restored order more quickly than one coconut water on a bench at the Savannah. The oil-company people didn't really care about the island's war but they did care about the island's black gold, so the American army came by air, the British by sea and the French just appeared. But by that time the family had packed and was ready for Canada, many other families would leave, the families of the haves who had been terrorized by the have-nots, the families who had bank accounts in Miami, the Cayman islands, Switzerland and even Dubai. They were leaving the island-city for a real metropolis as their Jamaican friends did long ago, and as their Jamaican friends were doing now – crime, devaluation, degradation, humiliation and deprivation were some of the reasons the islanders gave to the Canadians, the Americans, the British and the French as they knocked at their doors. And the doors opened for the lustful, the heretics, the gluttonous, the hypocrites, the falsifiers, the flatterers, the scandalous, the barrators, the traitors, the wrathful and the sullen. And the doors opened for the family, the father, the son, the mother and daughter, my old family, dear reader, had left me behind, but I had Virginia ready to lead me through the island, through its towns and cities and I had her lessons.

'Come, *chérie*, repeat after me, *ombre* is shade in Italian' – '*ombre* means shade'; '*notte* is night' – '*notte*, night'; '*partir* is to leave in French' – '*partir,* to leave'; '*rester,* to stay – *reposer,* to rest – *noche* is night, *dia* is day – they are both Spanish – *inferno* is hell in Italian – *paix* means peace' and so it would go until Virginia went away.

THE PARTY

I'll love you dear, dear I'll love you
Till China and Africa meet,
And the river jumps over the mountain
And the salmon sing in the street.
— W.H. Auden

Tricia shook her head and smiled, she was frying the *polori* balls for the party as she told Miss Alice the story of the piper-pimp and his two lady friends who had cleaned out Miss John's house while she was away, visiting her daughter 'in foreign'. They stole everything: fridge, stove, fans, dishes, glasses, pots, clothes, sheets, even Miss John's bras; the only things they left behind were her Bible, hymn book and two light bulbs. Everyone on Blackman Street heard the deep howl as the poor old lady walked into her house the night she returned from Brooklyn.

'Imagine those people buy them things knowing that it belong to their own neighbour. The piper and his lady friends have so much crack in their head 'fus they stupid enough to sell the things on the same street where they thief it.' Tricia laughed her high-pitched laugh, shook her head again, then took out another batch of golden *polori* balls and placed them on a sheet of neatly spread white napkins to absorb all the excess oil. The kitchen was filled with the delicious smell of *geera* and *massala*, frying in garlic, onions and yellow curry powder.

Alice smiled as she arranged the *samosas* and mini *rotis* she had ordered onto a large white platter. She loved to hear Tricia's stories; they had spent a lot of time this way, Tricia cooking and Alice listening to Tricia's stories about the Village.

'When they catch them I hear they put plenty licks on them in the Station. Sergeant Socks doh make joke, he doh stand for any stupidness, a real church man, every Sunday up in front, right next to Miss John and Father.' Tricia claimed that the piper confessed in less than half an hour and minutes later the police went into all the houses on the street to search for the stolen items.

You should see the neighbours, they so shame to show how much they buy from the piper. Ma John get everything back except the fridge, for some reason they can't find the fridge. No matter how much licks they put on the piper he doh want to tell Sergeant Socks who have the fridge. Five years they give him yes and they say Socks tell him to go and chill out in prison and see how many fridges he go steal there.'

Both Alice and Tricia giggled together. Alice felt lucky to have Tricia around, she could always tell a good story and make Alice laugh. Tricia lived on the same street as poor Miss John, Blackman Street, in an area they called 'the Village', five minutes by car from Alice's home, which the people from Tricia's Village called 'the Vale'. Every area in Pastora Valley had a name.

From the kitchen window Alice could see that the ashes were still falling even though the fires had stopped earlier that morning. They weren't the thick black ones that fell while the hills were still ablaze, but the thin ones, like strips of grey paper, light and weightless. Ashes had been falling in Pastora Valley for months, ever since the dry-season fires had begun in January. Sometimes they fell at night, or late evening, or even during the morning when the sun blazed through the Valley like a torch. But the ashes seldom fell at two o'clock in the afternoon. That year every field in the Valley, all the hills, the cocoa estates and the papaw fields were dry; the Valley was like a desert, shades of brown were everywhere – the leaves were a nut brown, the grass a golden brown, the earth a brown brown and the hills more black than brown. All the lawns (except the ones in the Vale where the owners used sprinklers illegally at night) had dried up. A thick layer of smoke often hovered over the Valley during the day and sometimes veiled all of the hills.

Alice went onto the covered part of the kitchen veranda where she usually had the birthday parties for Emma. She had to wait to see when the ashes would stop falling before she laid everything out on the long teak table she had inherited from her mother; when she was a child her mother would dress the table, the same teak table, for the beautiful Christmas lunch. Alice loved the weather at Christmas, the strong winds, the cool air; she missed the Christmas weather and everything that reminded her of her mother. 'Muggy' would be her mother's word for this weather, but for Alice it was just too hot, like some sort of hell.

Tricia covered all the bowls and platters with clear plastic wrap: the chocolate, coconut and vanilla fudge, the pink-and-white sugar cakes, the pinwheel cheese-paste sandwiches, the sausage rolls, the meat pies, the corn curls, the tortilla chips, the potato chips, the cup cakes and the huge bowl of lollipops. Tricia would wait before she put everything out, wait for the ashes to stop falling. Then Alice would dress the table with the alamanda and the fuchsia bougainvillea that grew along the edge of the front porch.

In the early mornings, before this terrible dry season, before Alice began her morning routine of filling Emma's lunch-kit or making breakfast for Emma and Scott, she would open the door and step onto the kitchen verandah; she loved the hills at the back of the house and the feel of that cool morning air on her face, the mist lifting like a curtain to reveal waves of sea-green hills. But these days, with all the fires, the early morning air felt as though the Valley had put on a thick woollen winter coat, so Alice stopped going outside. Except for this morning, for the first time in months, mainly because she couldn't sleep and mainly because it was Emma's birthday she opened her doors to the hills in the Valley but was disappointed at the sight of falling ashes.

Two nights before, Emma had run into Scott and Alice's bedroom with the deep scream children have when the fear sounds like a sharp pain. In between breaths, she told them she had heard seven gunshots in the hills (she had counted them), and she was sure that seven bandits were coming for her. Alice and Scott were already awake, they had heard the shots as well, there had been many more than seven; but to comfort Emma they lied and said that the boys in the Village were just 'bursting bamboo'. They let Emma get into bed and lie between them.

During the long night Scott tried to calm Emma as more sounds of shots entered the bedroom. Their sleep was broken at best; Scott got up a few times to check on the dogs; the older two, terrified of the noise, were huddled near the tool shed. In the morning Scott went to the Police Station to talk to Sergeant Socks. Since the dry season had begun Socks had stepped up the marijuana raids in the hills; he had already been featured twice on the evening news, standing in a field of marijuana holding his automatic weapon with heaps of ganja smoking in the background. Socks told Scott that a raid had taken place the night before to 'smoke out' two bandits who were hiding in the hills. Socks loved to use American phrases like 'smoke out', phrases he had heard on CNN. Before Scott left the Pastora Station, Sergeant Socks reassured him there was nothing to worry about and Scott reminded him about Emma's birthday party. An invitation Socks had always received ever since Alice and Scott moved into Pastora Valley seven years ago.

At 2:15 p.m. Alice was just about to call the Security Company when she saw the van pull up to the gate. The two guards came up to the camera perched high above the left stone pillar; they pressed the buzzer and spoke through the intercom. Looking into the small TV screen in the kitchen, Alice recognized the twins who provided the security for the dinner party they had had a month ago for Scott's parents' fortieth anniversary. This was a party she felt forced to have; she had never gotten along with Scott's mother, and with things so tense between Scott and herself the entire evening felt like hard work, with her acting the part of the contented wife and mother and smiling tight, wide smiles as the guests of honour were toasted again and again for forty more. That night Alice missed her mother more than ever; three years had already passed since she had lost her but the pain was still there, it was a nagging pain, numbed on busy days, paralysing on others, so Alice felt as though it would never go away and in a strange way she didn't want it too. With all of Scott's family at the anniversary party she felt lonelier than ever.

The owner of the Security Company, Scott's second cousin Jeffrey, was also invited to Emma's birthday party; his daughter Charlotte and Emma were the same age and in the same class at school. Alice opened the electric gates and the gleaming white pick-up with the dogs caged in the van's tray drove up the winding gravel path and parked at the side of the house. The dogs were trying to poke their muzzled snouts through the spaces in the wire cage. Luckily Scott had already put their four Rottweilers into the kennel. Only Netty, a skinny black mongrel, was still unleashed; she was a stray Alice had found two years ago at their beach house in La Fillette. Netty was friendly, harmless, protective and at times quite fierce, as though forever grateful for Alice's good deed. As soon as Scott saw the van he put down the weed-wacker and went towards the security guards. His T-shirt was soaking with sweat; he had spent most of the morning with their gardener, Ricky, cutting down the dry bush around the edges of the property.

Alice was staring at Scott; just looking at him made her angry; he could be smiling, walking, drinking a cup of coffee, playing with Emma or the dogs and she would feel like slapping and scraping him over and over again. They had been having the same fight for the last two years; things would calm down for a month or so, sometimes more, and then something would trigger it and it would start all over again. The months of counselling, the vacations to the Bahamas, London and Paris, the separation, the short-lived reconciliation, the brief honeymoons, none of it could get rid of the intense desire she had on bad days to hurt him badly, the way he had hurt her when she found out about his screwing that bitch Nalini. How many times had she warned Scott about Nalini? About what her friends called the Caroni Complex. Nalini was exactly one of those country Indians who had left the cane fields to find a sugar daddy in town. Her over-friendly manner, her willingness to work overtime, even on

Sundays, her tacky, skanky outfits. But Scott never listened to Alice or at least preferred not to.

'Eric. William. How's it going?' Scott shook their hands. Scott was always very good with names and with people; his job as director of the sales department in his father's Marine Equipment Company demanded it.

'Afternoon Mr Charles,' they both said in unison, in the same polite tone, 'Sorry to be late, we had to wait for the dogs,' Eric continued.

'No problem.' Scott walked towards the kennel; both sets of dogs were now going crazy, snarling and barking at each other. 'Take your set around to the back to calm these down a little; we have a horse coming too.' Scott didn't see the need to have horse rides, a Bouncy Castle and two children's make-up artists all for a six year old's party, but he was still doing as much as he could to keep Alice calm, if not happy, today. He tried to convince himself that she had actually forgiven him for the night he had spent with his former secretary Nalini two years ago; that one-night stand, that one, drunk, fucked-up fuck had cost him two years and counting. Scott tried to convince himself that things would get back on track, the way they were before Nalini. Early on, after he was cornered by Alice and like an idiot confessed, he felt like running away, taking Emma and moving out because he couldn't take the torture of the never-ending interrogations, the silences that could last for days, or the constant badgering, the crying, the screaming, that feeling of apprehension, of tension, from the moment he walked into the door on evenings. One night when he decided he couldn't keep paying for his crime any longer, he drove off leaving Alice screaming on the verandah, holding Emma. He stayed at his cousin Jeffrey's house for two days. Alice never called. But all Scott could think about was Alice and Emma and so he went back. Scott knew then that Alice would have to be the one to leave because he felt even more battered and broken away from her and from his Emma. They had known each other since high school, for goodness sake, but there were sides to Alice that Scott knew he would probably never understand.

Beyond their own mess, she carried a sadness inside her, probably as a result of losing her father when she was only six, Emma's age. To survive, Scott tried hard not to think about what he had done or even Alice's unhappiness.

'Plenty bush fires up here, Mr Charles?' Eric asked.

'Boy, endless, and the ashes only just settling down, earlier today they were falling like rain.'

Eric and William both gave a pleasant grunt, then worked quickly to get their two pit bulls out of the van's tray away from Mr Charles's dogs and immediately began to patrol the perimeter of the backyard. They wore the usual uniform: black cargo pants tucked into black high-top boots, black short-sleeved shirts with two pockets on either side, guns in their gun holders and wraparound black shades. They weren't the typical blue-black, stocky, muscular security guards that most companies used; Eric and William had light-brown skin, were slim and not very tall. They looked more like bank clerks, Alice thought, looking out at them from the kitchen window, but according to Jeffrey they were his best men.

The dogs finally settled down but all the noise had woken up Emma. Alice heard Emma's familiar scream for Tricia. They were all trying to let her nap as close to party time as possible. Although 3.30 was the time on the invitations, Alice knew that most of the guests wouldn't arrive before four. Tricia had just stepped into the backyard to pick some dill and a little rosemary for the yogurt dip that Alice had taught her to make.

Trish, Emma's up, I'll do the dip if you get her ready.'

'Yes Miss Alice.' Tricia picked another sprig of rosemary and then hurried back inside. She washed her hands in the large kitchen sink, dried them with the towel on the counter and left Alice opening the containers of plain yogurt for the dip. Alice didn't look up at Tricia when she said, 'The dress for the party is on the bed. Put her hair in a bun, she'll want to leave it out but it will get too messy, thanks Trish.' Tricia saw Eric and William walk by the perimeter of the porch; she knew them; they acknowledged her with a nod and moved the dogs away.

Tricia's only son, Tony, used to work for Mr Jeffrey's Security Company as well, but the long hours, the good chance of being shot by some show-off bandit and the minimum-wage pay check made him leave. Things only got worse after he left the job; he started liming with a group of young Muslimeen who claimed to be doing community work in the Village; everyone knew they were selling drugs and looking for new recruits. Tricia and Tony fought daily about all the time he spent with them, until one day she came home from work to a neatly made bed and a note. It said that he believed that Islam was the path to his new God, Allah, and that she shouldn't worry because he would be taken care of by his Muslimeen brothers on their compound deep in the Sans Souci hills. Tricia could do nothing to get him back; her only consolation was that he wasn't in Sergeant Sock's area anymore; the last two Muslimeen youths from the Village (boys no more than seventeen) were shot dead by Sergeant Socks right in front of Woo's Grocery. Socks and his men accused them of robbery and the attempted kidnapping of Mr Woo himself. No one disagreed, not even Mr Woo, even though everyone knew that Frank Woo was burying his first cousin in Arouca that very Saturday. The rumour was that Socks shot those boys to send a message to their boss, the Imam on the Sans Souci compound, who owed Socks a lot of money.

These days Tricia saw her son once a month. Tony, now Hassan Ali, would pull up to her gate in the Village in his shiny black Sentra, never without two other 'brothers' from his youth group; he'd blow the horn and she would come out. Tricia's neighbours in the Village always paid attention when they saw the black car with the young Muslimeens driving up the street; if mothers were inside their homes they peeped through their curtains and kept their young boys inside, but the young men liming on the corner hailed the car as it passed as though it were a chariot carrying kings. Later in the day when Sergeant Socks came to make his rounds they hailed his jeep in the same way.

Tony never got further than the gate to mutter an 'assalam-o-alaikum', then a 'hello ma', handing her an envelope before he got back into the car with his brothers in their black shades, white robes and white toupees. She took the money, never asking where it came from (things were just too hard now to think about that), half for her, half for Tony's child-mother and their baby girl, Fatima. In the early days after Tony left, Tricia would lie on her bed at night and weep holding her stomach like a child with a terrible stomach ache but now she just took the money and thanked her God that her son was still alive. Tony, he was her only begotten son. She had had hopes for that boy; the teachers used to say how bright he was and she had worked hard to give him what she could, because for most of his life it had just been the two of them.

Upstairs Tricia had managed to get a still drowsy Emma into the dress from her godparents, Jeffrey and his wife Kathy; it was a deep pink, embroidered with small yellow-and-blue flowers around the sleeve, neckline and hem. Emma's godparents had bought it on their last cruise to Mexico. Emma often resisted any suggestions Alice made about clothes, but she always accepted Tricia's without a fuss. So Alice usually had Tricia dress her for special occasions.

Alice put the dip in the fridge and went upstairs to Emma's room. From the doorway she saw Tricia combing Emma's thick, curly brown hair; hair Emma hated because it wasn't straight and smooth like Barbie's or silky and straight like her cousin Charlotte's. They were facing the window not the door; Emma's room had one of the best views in the house; in the rainy season the two sets of large sliding windows opened up to the thick green Valley hills and in the dry season, if there weren't too many fires, the hills were orange and yellow from the immortelle and poui trees.

Alice looked at Tricia from the doorway. They were only a year apart, but Tricia was already a grandmother at forty. She had on an old floral dress Alice had given her a few years ago and a pair of Alice's old slippers. The angle of Tricia's body exposed a thin leg that looked dry, black and powdery; the heel of her foot was flaking, the sole was thick and yellow, her body looked old but her voice was that of a young girl's. Alice often wondered what it would have been like if, in another life, things were turned around and she were the one working for Tricia in Tricia's old dress with her dry, black skin, her kinky black hair, her two-room home and this job, bringing up somebody else's child. When Emma was a baby, Tricia used to sing hymns to her from her church while she brushed her hair, but these last few months, ever since her son joined the Muslimeen, Alice noticed a change in Tricia. She still laughed when she told Alice stories about the Village but whenever Tricia thought she was alone Alice could see the sadness in her.

'You going to behave a nice girl at the party,' Tricia said as she pulled Emma's hair into a perfect bun. Emma nodded.

'So tell Trish who coming to your party?'

Emma began her list, 'Charlotte, Juliette, Jean-Paul, Emily-Louise, Izzy, Tara…' Alice walked away quietly, still hearing them chatting; she had hoped that the distance she felt between herself and Emma would get better with time, but it had only gotten worse and what Scott had done didn't help. For some strange reason she had passed some of the anger she felt for Scott on to Emma. Or maybe she was always jealous of the way Scott treated Emma, he was so gentle with her, always trying his best not to hurt her. But it wasn't just Scott, Alice had always envied mothers, like her mother, like Tricia, who felt this closeness to their children right away and knew how to make it grow.

As Alice passed the large glass window along the corridor she noticed the twins, Eric and William, standing with their dogs like statues on either side of the entrance; by the time she got to her bedroom and looked again they had disappeared.

Alice knew that this was not the best time to have a party. There had been so many kidnappings in the last few months that many of Emma's classmates had bodyguards as drivers. Only a year ago, if a parent couldn't make it, they would send the housekeeper or sitter; now they sent a bodyguard. Good security had to be provided at the parties, otherwise the parents would think twice about coming or sending their child. She didn't like having the parties, never did, even though she tried her best to hide that fact from both Scott and Emma with her wide smiles and supreme organization. She didn't like being inspected by the other mothers. In the beginning she tried to make an extra effort to keep up, spending the day at the salon, buying new outfits for herself, Emma and even Scott. But lately what she wore to a birthday party seemed to matter less and less to her. Her standard khaki Capri and a black T-shirt would have to do today.

When Scott and Alice first moved into Pastora seven years ago, having grown up in areas where grotesque sprawling houses covered most of the land, they were excited by all the green fields with the Buffalypso, the old cocoa estates, and even the fires in the hills around the Vale at night. Sometimes the Valley would burn for days and nights but after one heavy downpour of white rain it could renew itself again, with fresh razor grass reclaiming the burnt earth in what seemed like minutes. At night, during the dry season, they sometimes sat outside on the verandah to look at fires; orange cinders sparkled against a pitch-black night with silvery blue stars and a thick, milky moon. The black hills looked like volcanoes, sending streams of lava into the Valley below. Once, Alice even tried to write a poem about the Valley at night using all the same words: silvery blue stars, milky moon and streams of lava, but she never finished it.

Everyone said that this dry season was different not just in the Valley but all over the island. There were fires everywhere on the hills, even along the highways with flames sometimes licking the cars as they drove by. Hot, hazy mornings exposed the damage done the night before; the earth looked like chunks of coal, and ashes, like mounds of salt, were everywhere. The local Venezuelan psychic said that the island was being punished for all the terrible crimes: 'De kidnapping, de murder, de chile abuse and de drogues, taking over.' The leader of the largest Pentecostal church on the island, Pastor Henry, pleaded with the entire nation to 'stop allowing evil to take over our bodies, our minds, our hearts and our souls because Judgment Day was fast approaching and we didn't have much time'; he had seen in a dream the horsemen of the Apocalypse. Catholics, Anglicans, Hindus and Moslems all called for a national day of prayer. The Government promised more policemen on the streets, help from the army and even more help from Venezuela's *Guardia Nacional* to patrol our 'drug-infested waters'. Alice and Scott had even discussed leaving the island but they didn't want to end up in Miami like so many of their friends.

The phone rang. Alice heard Scott pick it up downstairs. After the call he came upstairs and gently shut the door of their bedroom. Alice glanced at the clock on the bedside table; it was already 2:35 p.m.

'That was Jeffery on the phone, they're not coming, Kathy is too upset. Apparently they tried to take the Clarke boy early yesterday morning, around 3 a.m. They followed him from The Club. When he slowed down at the traffic lights before the turn off into Golf View, they tried to grab him and push him into a car…'

'So what does that have to do with not bringing Charlotte?'

'Kathy is worried.'

'About what?'

'I just said *what,* they took the Clarke boy.'

'So what does that have to do with Charlotte coming to Emma's party?'

'I don't know, the Clarkes live on the same street, quite close to them.'

'I know all that but I still don't see what it has to do with Charlotte. Kathy is so damn jealous of everything. What does she think? That they going to take her? Or her lovely Charlotte? She thinks that they're really in the same league as the Clarke's?'

Scott kept silent, stared at her for a moment, then went into their bathroom. Alice heard the swish of the sliding door, then the shower. She sat down on her bed, then stretched out on a cushion and stared at the wooden rafters above. It had begun. The party was beginning to unravel; all that planning and now Emma would be disappointed. It was no secret that Kathy and Alice didn't like each other. Alice found that Kathy was superficial, snotty and stupid. And it didn't help that Kathy's family had always been friendly with Scott's family, or that Alice felt that Scott's mother would have preferred Kathy for Scott, or that Kathy was undeniably pretty in that obvious sort of way. And the fact that Scott had spent those two nights at Jeffrey and Kathy's house when things were at their worst made Alice hate Kathy even more, because now Kathy probably knew about the affair although Scott swore he never told her. Once, early in their marriage, Scott told Alice that maybe she was just a little jealous of Kathy; after that, Alice didn't talk to Scott for a week, so now Scott avoided talking about Kathy unless, like today, it was unavoidable.

Scott got out of the shower, put on his jeans, white polo shirt and a pair of sneakers. He left Alice still lying on the bed staring at the ceiling. He knew better than to say anything more about Kathy. Things seemed to be getting worse not better; he didn't know how to talk to her anymore, so he usually agreed with her or said very little. He could see them moving away from each other in slow motion, like two people in a corny, Bollywood film; he had been looking at this film for a while and now he had no idea how to get the two people back to that point close to the beginning where they seemed happy.

Alice watched Scott leave the room without saying a word. She could hear Charlotte going down the stairs with Tricia. She could hear the dogs barking at Eric and William. She could even hear Emma's sweet giggle. But Alice, still smelling of curry, was tired, very tired. So she closed her eyes for what seemed like seconds; when she heard the buzzer for the gate it startled her; she had dropped off to sleep. She got up and walked to her bedroom window. It was Mr Xavier with the horse for the party. The gate opened. She watched old Mr Xavier get back into his rickety pick-up, pulling the horse in another tray and slowly drive up to the house. Scott and Ricky were already there to help him.

Suddenly she had the terrible thought of no children turning up for the party. But they would come; many had already RSVP'd; it was just Charlotte's absence and Kathy's desire to ruin everything, just to spite her, that troubled her now. Alice didn't want to think about the Clarke boy. Two young children had been kidnapped in the last month; the first had been tortured and beaten to death with a cricket bat, but he was the grandson of a well-known drug runner; the second child, a casino owner's son, again with a potential drug link, was simply shot in the head and had his hands cut off, a sign, the newspapers said, that the family had owed or stolen money. Both children, as horrible as their deaths were, came from what everyone called the drug coast. But the Clarkes, they all knew the Clarkes; they were a wealthy family, quietly so; they owned some of the most beautiful property on the island, bought for a song by Grandpa Clarke long before anyone imagined that those areas would ever be worth anything or be populated. The Clarkes were rich but not from drugs. No one was immune anymore, not from this plague that seemed to be spreading so fast.

Faster than even Alice had expected. Last week on Alice's way home after picking up Emma from her school, she thought she was being followed by a black sedan with at least four heads in it; the car followed her from the moment she turned onto the main road all the way onto the main Valley road. Alice wanted to call Scott on her cell phone but Emma was in the car and she didn't want to scare her. So she drove, pretending to listen to a new song Emma had been taught at school and tried her best to keep an eye on the black car following her. As she passed the Pastora Valley Police Station she slowed down. Emma asked why, but Alice told her that she just wanted to give Sergeant Socks an invitation to her birthday party. As soon as she turned into the Police Station, the black sedan zoomed ahead. The policemen on duty told her that Sergeant Socks was out on a 'Recon'. She left the invitation for Socks and drove away. Everyone in the Vale invited Socks to their parties since they all depended on his goodwill to keep, as Socks said, 'evil at bay'.

In fact with each month Socks was becoming more and more famous, not just for catching kidnappers or finding ganja fields all over the island, but recently for his cocaine discoveries. Only last week Socks and his men had found packs of cocaine brought in with the tide onto a beach in a remote fishing village on the north coast, the drug coast. The Minister of National Security and

Socks were featured together on the front page of *The Daily News* after that incredible find; the Minister was quoted as saying that the country needed more policemen like Socks: 'We Need More Socks!' the headline read. Some months ago another newspaper hinted at a different side to Socks, suggesting police brutality, strong ties to the drug world, and questioned how he was able to find all those marijuana fields. But questions on the island were never pursued; it didn't matter which government party was in power. The last time Alice had seen Socks he was talking to a neighbour at the front gate; the Hernandezes had had a break-in while vacationing in London. Socks was his usual animated self, arms flailing and gesturing as he usually did with his thumb cocked and index finger pointed like a gun.

It was 3:20 p.m. Alice didn't want to get up. Her tiredness never seemed to leave her now; it was always there like the heat and the ashes in this never-ending dry season. But she knew it was more than tiredness; a feeling of deadness had taken over in the last couple of months which made it harder to do the things she had managed to do before: taking care of Emma, going for a walk, pulling up weeds in the garden, calling a friend. She didn't feel like going down stairs to greet the guests, she didn't feel like going to her own daughter's birthday party. On the outside she pretended to worry about the details, the little things, but inside her head was filled with bigger worries: the shootings in the hills, the abused children on the front pages of the newspapers, the kidnapped bodies found lying in gutters, the disease-ridden prisons, the police beatings, the street children, the skeletal beggars and everything Scott had taken away from her. Alice could not imagine a change, not in herself and especially not in this place she called home. She wanted to leave her life, the beautiful house, the Valley; she wanted to sleep but instead she got up, dressed, washed her face, brushed her hair, put on lipstick, mascara, perfume and went down stairs before the first guest for the party arrived.

THE WARD

We lived there, Michael and me. The others were our guests. They came, they left, they spent a night, a week, a month, but they always went home. A he, a she, a friend, a granny, a tanty – somebody would always come for them. Even if the somebody never came on the exact day or at the exact time they said they would, somebody came. Sometimes they said they would come at six on Monday and they didn't show their face until nine on Wednesday, but they still came. And from the moment the guests knew they were going home, they would start to talk about 'home', as though 'home' meant coconut ice-cream, chocolate cake and jokes all day. They didn't say anything about the usual kicks, blows and elbows to the head. 'Home' was mangoes for breakfast, lunch, dinner and breakfast the next day. It was mangoes everyday that mangoes were in season. 'Home' was carrying buckets of water to wash down the stinking backyard, full of green watery lumps from all the mangoes that were eaten. And if there was no water, 'home' was covering your nose and trying to find a clear spot, without flies, where you could stoop over to empty your empty belly.

Once in a while, we had a foreign guest like the little American boy called Baby Bob. Baby Bob's mother sat beside his crib hour after hour, for four days and three nights. She never left his crib except to go to the bathroom or to stretch her legs for exactly five minutes when a shift changed and there was a White Dress she thought she could trust. Baby Bob's flesh was loose, yellowish-pink, wrinkled, salty and scaly like a an old man's. The White

Dresses told the mother that he was dehydrated, that he would be better soon. But among themselves, they whispered other things. 'Malyeux', they said, which meant someone had given the baby the evil eye. The American didn't know how to protect the child with jumbie beads. The White Dresses said that she loved the child too much, and sometimes God, being a jealous god, punished mothers for loving their babies more than Him. When they couldn't find a vein as they poked and poked needles into the back of Baby Bob's tiny hands, they muttered that the curse was strong. Little by little, Baby Bob's skin started to fill out; he began to get fatter and fatter. But as the air filled up Baby Bob's body, the mother grew smaller and smaller. He sucked all the milk, blood and air out of her body from the tiny hole in her small breasts.

Some guests never made it back from the Big House. We saw them leave, attached to drips, respirators or whatever. They never came back. We knew, Michael and me, that once their crib or bed had been stripped of its sheets we would never see them again. The bed was soon ready for another guest. We had our own beds, Michael and me. They changed the sheets once a week, whether or not any 'accidents' took place. And with Michael, 'accidents' took place almost every night. He couldn't speak, at least not their language, but I knew when he had had a bad night, when his dreams had taken him to that bright white place where shadows chase you, where you scream a scream that never comes, with mouth and eyes frozen open. I had been to that bright white place where you try to run from shadows, but your legs are filled with cement. Then the scream finally comes; it doesn't sound like a scream but more like a deep grunt that has come up all the way from your toes. Michael had these dreams all the time. During these dreams he had his 'accidents'. They smelt like a rotten-egg-red-bean fart, they didn't bother me; it was Michael's smell and that was all.

In the morning, at 6 a.m., just as the new shift of White Dresses came in, they bathed us. Whether or not we were still asleep, they shook us, made us walk about the room to 'put some heat in our bodies' and then they took us two by two to the shower. If there was no water, we had to bathe out of buckets. The water was always cold because early mornings on the hill were chilly. Pouring that melted ice over our naked bodies first thing in the morning made some of the new guests cry out. But we were used to it; we never uttered a sound even though our bodies shook all over. Then we were dressed as fast as possible in whatever was in the cupboard that could fit, wasn't too big or falling off, or too tight to go over the head or the bottom. We lost a lot of buttons because the regulars never brought their own clothes; they knew about the extra clothes in the cupboard. Usually the White Dresses used tape to hold our shirts together.

After the bath, there was breakfast on the long table in the middle of the big room. The big room was long and lean. At the head was the fat bow-legged desk where a White Dress always sat. On the desk was a phone, a lamp and a long cream book that said how many guests there were, what medication each guest needed and when last they got it. The cupboard with all the clothes was right next to the desk so that the White Dresses could 'throw an eye on it', because sometimes the regulars tried to steal our clothes.

Along the walls of the big room were the beds and cribs. There were six beds and five cribs; each one had a number written in black on the wall. We all (all of us except Michael and the guests who were confined to their beds) ate breakfast, lunch and dinner on the long table in the middle of the room. It was a low table for small children with baby chairs and benches painted in chipped pink, yellow or blue paint. The table was perfect for a guest under three feet but anyone else would feel like a giant unable to get their knees under the table. The table's white-and-red checkered plastic cover was always sticky no matter how many times they wiped it. And the more they wiped it, the more it would stink, like the damp mouldy clothes we wore, like the cold, grey, concrete, urine-smelling floor which no amount of mopping or Dettol could cover.

They tried to brighten the cream walls of the big room with fat, pink numbers and Sesame Street characters like Big Bird, Cookie Monster, Grover and Burt. But the paintings looked nothing like the real muppets we saw on TV: Big Bird looked like a monster, Burt had vampire teeth and Cookie Monster's eyes made the babies cry. They put up a sign, 'Welcome, We Love You', over the empty bookcase at the other end of the room, but nothing, not even a sunny day on the hill, could brighten that room.

Breakfast was the first meal they served. We always had two choices. On Fridays, Saturdays and Sundays, when there was the most traffic – mothers dropping off the regulars, the Head White Dress checking up on her workers and guests, fathers visiting, then disappearing again for months – with all the people around, we had the special breakfast: two pieces of damp, margarine-covered toast, one oily, sunnyside-up egg and two small sausages. We washed it all down with a cup of cocoa made with sweetened condensed milk. The rest of the week we had a bowl of Cream of Wheat or Quaker Oats floating in watery milk with a cup of bitter cocoa. Michael never had meals with us because he 'made too much confusion'. Once or twice they tried him at the table, but one morning his sharp teeth punctured a little girl's ankle. It was his last chance. After that, Michael ate alone in the back room, sitting on the floor with one ankle tied with a rope to a crib leg. A White Dress was always around to keep an eye on him. He ate with his hands and much of the meal was tossed around on the floor.

After breakfast we were allowed to stroll, never run, around the room. The faded, tired, rose curtains were drawn. The louvres were opened to 'let in the sea breeze' and to let us see the black hills and the light-green water. For the regulars, this was the best part of the day: the bath was over with, their bellies were full and they didn't have a single chore but to walk around the room and look at the sea. They didn't care that they couldn't go outside; being outside was not something they wanted. When they were at home in their shaking, leaking sheds, they were forced to go outside to collect water, to wash clothes, to 'pass water' and to sell limes. Outside meant nothing but hot sun and hard work. But for Michael and me, it was everything. We longed to go outside, just to feel the brown grass instead of the cold, grey floor. Happiness was to see nothing around us, no Big Bird, no numbers, no White

Dresses, just the hills and the sea. Michael longed to go outside even more than I did. He howled and howled in the mornings, begging to go outside. But the White Dresses never understood; they just gave Michael his medicine. Then he would move slowly, sadly and soon fall asleep. He missed most mornings, waking up for lunch.

Christmas was one of the few times we were allowed outside. The choirs came and sang carols on the lawn. The Big Hats visited and took us to the Zoo or the Botanical Gardens. The Big Hats brought shiny gifts: crisp clothes, gold buttons, fresh, new colouring books, packs of sharpened bright colours of wax, and blue tins filled with chocolate, sugar and butter biscuits. The White Dresses grabbed all the gifts, thanking the Big Hats over and over again. All the clothes and colouring books were put in the cupboard and bookcase, but the next morning they had disappeared. The White Dresses would take home the new clothes and most of the colouring books for their own children and ate the biscuits themselves. They usually saved a book or two and some colouring pencils for Michael and me but I always got Michael's because he would try to eat the paper and crayons.

From the back of the room where we slept, I could see the entrance; I knew every crack in that road, every tree, all the cars, I made it part of our world. Through the louvres, I saw the ambulances bringing in the new guests. I saw the huge, flat-bottomed American taxis bringing in the fat boiling sausages in their black glasses to see the view from the top of the hill. Later in the evening as the sun set, lovers from the town walked up the hill, hugging, kissing, poking, grabbing and pinching each other. The ladies wore short, black, lace dresses and white high heels. The men wore black pants, white shirts and ties. Thinking no one was looking, the men would try to put their hands up the black, lace dresses; the ladies would giggle, say 'stop it', but didn't move away the hands searching under their dresses. I saw them and told Michael everything. The louvres in the back room were too high for him to see outside because Michael, although he was the tallest of us all, could only crawl. His arms were longer than his

legs, his head was too heavy and too wide for his shoulders, and
his knees were always bent. The White Dresses seldom let him
out of his crib, but when they untied his ankle and let him crawl,
the first thing he would do was howl, a big, long, wide howl, like
the howler monkeys at the Zoo. He would try to stand up but he
would always fall down; then he would squat and do his howler-
monkey walk with his arms swishing at his sides, grazing the
floor. He would go to the bathroom, drink the water in the toilet
bowl, take off his oversized diaper and play with the long, hard,
brown roll inside. His time out of the crib never lasted long. I did
tricks, made monkey-faces, anything to keep him out of trouble
but it never worked. The White Dresses would soon put him back
in his crib and give him more medicine. I looked out of the
louvres in the back room and told him about the cars coming with
the new guests. I told him about the stories I had read. I showed
him the pictures I had drawn. But the medicine made Michael
sleep before I could finish telling him everything.

I didn't have to take any medicine to make me sleep. As long
as I stayed out of trouble, the White Dresses let me roam around
the rooms all day. I had a copy book where I wrote down
everything: the bed and the cribs that had guests, the name of each
guest, the length of time they stayed with us, and all the TV
shows, because the TV was on all the time. It was in a big, black
cage suspended above the empty bookcase. The White Dresses
turned it on at 9 a.m. for 'Sesame Street' and left it on until 9 p.m.
when the curtains were drawn and all the lights switched off
except for the lamp on the desk where the White Dress on duty
sat. But even when there were no longer American voices in the
air, there was never really any silence. Especially at night, especially when the shift changed at 9 p.m. The White Dresses who
took that shift didn't want to do anything else but sleep. There
were usually just two of them: one would sit at the desk for half
the night and the other would lie curled up on the big, cushioned
chair in the pantry.

At around 2 a.m. they would change places. Sometimes they
even unplugged the phone. Often, the one at the desk would put

on headphones and listen to music to drown out the cries the babies made at night. And the babies always cried when they had nightmares or when their diapers were so full that the sheets were soaked and their thighs were covered in baby mess. Some babies cried because their covers had come off and they were cold; some just wanted to feel a warm body or hear a warm, creamy voice. But the Night White Dresses seldom moved or even looked up from their desk. Michael howled as much as the babies. At night, with the light from the street lamp filtering into our room, I could see Michael's huge saucer-mouth, his cracked front teeth and his brownish-pink gums. His eyes were black holes, he had no eyebrows, he had a tuft of black, fuzzy hair on the top of his head and his ears stuck out at the sides. The White Dresses used to say that Michael was so ugly he was beautiful. But to me, Michael was not beautiful, he was not ugly; at night, Michael was just a howler.

Once, a baby boy came to the hill with a swollen belly after having eaten foam from the mattress in a crib. The foam had expanded in the baby boy's stomach after he drank water. The baby boy bawled and they took him to the Big House. Michael had eaten foam as well, not because he was hungry like the baby boy but because Michael ate everything. His saucer-mouth was always open; it caught flies, mosquitoes and cockroaches. His giant crib was left empty because he sucked up everything that was ever placed, thrown or pitched inside. He slept without a blanket, pillow or sheet. A huge howler in a giant crib cage.

My small bed had bars on either side, my pencil and copybook under my pillow, a pack of crayons and four colouring books under my mattress. They were mine. The White Dresses gave me colouring books and a pack of crayons every Christmas. I took my time to colour every spot on every page, so besides the black outline of Snow White, Goldilocks or Hansel and Gretel, every other space had been filled in blue, pink and yellow, my favourite colours. The colouring books, the crayons, the copybook and the pencil were mine. I didn't come with them. I came, the White Dresses claim, wearing nothing but a dirty, yellow-stained dia-per. A lady dropped me off, maybe my mother or her sister; the

White Dresses didn't know. In the beginning, they said, I was just a regular because the woman would drop me off before working nights. At first, she would make up some illness; she would say I had had a fever all night, or diarrhoea or headaches. She said she would come back in the morning to get me. Then, after a while, she wouldn't even make up a problem, just ask the White Dress in charge to keep me for the weekend. One Friday night, she dropped me off as usual but never came back. The White Dresses believe she went away with one of her tourist customers. Maybe he offered her a better life, where she didn't have to work at night. Maybe she wasn't even my mother at all; maybe my real mother left me with this woman. I never asked about her but the White Dresses always told me the story whenever the question of birthdays came up. They didn't even know when I was born. I had no papers. They didn't know my father's name. They didn't even know the woman's name.

I didn't remember anyone's name. I was too small or maybe somewhere I knew they would all leave me one day on the hill so I didn't need to remember their names. My home was the hill. The White Dresses were my keepers. They dressed me, fed me, taught me my colours, my ABCs and my 123s. Michael, the howler monkey, was my brother. The regulars were our friends. They had mothers or just women who came and left. These women wore short, black skirts, which stuck to their big, round bottoms like glue. Sometimes their skirts were so short their red panties peeped out when they sat or bent. Sometimes they didn't wear panties at all and all you could see was a bushy black hole. They had greasy faces, red lips, long, black, horsehair wigs and silver dust above their black eyes. They wore short tight tops, showing off their flat, long, dry breasts and their jelly bellies. Underneath their arms were hairy and sour. Their fingernails and toenails were painted in chipped, red nail polish. Their legs were round, thick, black and greasier than their shiny faces. They were beautiful, more beautiful than the hills or the sea. She was probably beautiful too, the one who forgot to pick me up, the one who forgot to tell them my name.

THE BOULEVARD

Father Petri used to say to us in school before we began an essay, 'Boys, start your composition with a strong frame, so that you can fatten it with a fleshy middle and the end will come when it will come.' Now what Father Petri meant was a mystery to me. The end will come when it will come. In Mamma's stories, the end was always this, 'Crick-crack', and her beginnings always were, 'Once upon a time'. So I begin like Mamma. Once upon a time, I lived opposite a king. He was A.C. Miller, the king of my Boulevard, even if Trinidad stopped having kings a long time ago.

The Boulevard was wider than any street in Port-of-Spain. It had the Queen's Park Savannah at its head and a cemetery at its feet. On one side there were the French Creole houses, big and white, with high walls and long cars. On my side the houses were much smaller and usually grey. I lived next door to Mr Epps's Parlour and Roti Shop. It didn't bother me too much that I was on the other side because when I told the boys in St Xavier's that I lived on the Boulevard opposite A.C. Miller their bottom lip fell. Miller owned half the town. I knew all about the house of Miller from Mamma because she was friendly with their best cook. She told Mamma all the French Creole *komesse*, who was seeing who on the side, who had a big belly, what this one had on and so on and so on. She told Mamma about the two old aunts living in the house and the two young nieces. The servants called one of the aunts Old May and everyone knew Old May's story. Once upon a time a young boy pretended to love the old lady. He gave her dresses and shoes or whatever young men give old ladies when they say they love them. But when all of Old May's money was spent, her young lover ran off with the gardener's daughter. Poor Old May lost her North. She would leave the Boulevard at five in the morning and wander around the wharf, swearing at all the young men she saw and wearing the dresses one on top of the other, looking for her young lover. One day, Old May just dropped dead, probably dying from the heartache or the heat, so my mother said. Crick-crack.

The other aunt from the house of Miller played the piano and sang after dinner. The two young nieces were always stuck up in the house. Robin, my best friend (Mr Epps's son), and I called the younger one Tambrun because she was so sour. The older one smiled more, but Tambrun was easier on the eyes. To tell you the truth, Tambrun's eyes were like clear green Tobago water, so pretty against her honey-coloured skin they made me want to marry her. I studied A.C. Miller carefully, how he walked in his stiff grey suits, how he sat so upright in his car, and how he waved his hand like a king at the yard-boy, Ali, as he closed the gate. I studied A.C. Miller because one day I was going to walk into the house and take Tambrun with me.

At night I prayed, asking God to set me tasks to prove myself worthy of being like A.C. Miller so that the family would accept me, even though I lived on the other side of the Boulevard. One night I dreamt I was riding around the Savannah with my hands in the air, singing our national anthem. The next morning I realized that God had given me a sign; soon Tambrun would be mine.

Every afternoon after school I would sit on my wall, waiting to see if Tambrun and her sister would go into their yard to play. At least twice a week I was lucky and saw her. But two weeks passed without even a glimpse of Tambrun. So that afternoon I headed for the Savannah where I could practise my sacred task of riding no hands and singing the anthem. And God was good to me. There she was, my beautiful Tambrun, walking around the Queen's Park Savannah with the Millers' hound Felix, a huge black Alsatian that Robin and I called the wolf. Mamma once told us the Miller cook said that Felix almost killed a peeping tom outside Old May's window. They couldn't get the dog's teeth out of the boy's flesh until Tambrun said, 'Felix, sit.' So as I got closer to Tambrun and Felix, I reminded myself to stay calm.

I rode with one foot touching the ground, the other on the pedal. Then I realized that coming from the rear might startle Felix, so I cut through the Savannah dirt path, stopped four benches ahead of them and pretended to take a stone out of my tyre. When they were close enough for me to notice Tambrun's white socks covering her thin ankles, I stood up. I heard myself say hello. Tambrun smiled but kept walking in true Miller fashion, nose in the air, eyes straight ahead. They were about to take the bend when I lost control and shouted, 'Stop.' She did.

'Are you A.C. Miller's niece?'

'Yes.'

I had nothing prepared after that.

'Nice dog,' I said.

'Thanks. His name's Felix.' Saliva was dripping from Felix's mouth.

We just stood there, looking at Felix. Then all of a sudden there was a stream of cars and the sound of their horns. One car had a giant-sized loudspeaker on the roof, blasting Indian music. A long black American car passed covered with flowers. It was the bride's car. I saw the wedding procession as another sign, which gave me the courage to turn to Tambrun and say, 'My name is Anthony J. Harris. I live close to you on the Boulevard.'

'Yes, I know,' she said and walked away with Felix.

I thought the cars from the wedding had gone past us but then came one more, blowing its horn frantically, hustling to catch up with the others.

My legs were so weak from the encounter I had to sit down. 'Tambrun knows me,' I kept saying to myself. Before riding home, I went round the Savannah one more time. I raised my hands as I passed Tambrun and Felix, and began to sing our national anthem. By the time I got to the end of the Boulevard, I was going so fast I almost crashed into Mr Epps's old Volkswagen. He was lying under the car, swearing at the engine, calling her a *jammet*, a *hoe*, a bitch and a *chabine*. His body was buried underneath the car. All I could see was his fat toes in a pair of rubber slippers.

'Blasted children,' he shouted. 'Don't know how to take your damn time.'

'Sorry, Mr Epps.'

Robin was not in the yard so I decided to head for the cemetery. There was no better place to play cricket, not even in the Savannah. And all of us on my side of the street knew this. It was the cricket season, and we, the Boulevard Bowlers, had a game in two weeks against the Corbeau Town Boys. They were supposed to have the best twelve-year-old fast bowler in the land: Johnny Khan, whom they called JCB (Johnny Can Bowl). They said he was another Sobers and would soon be batting better than Lara. So I rode to the cemetery, even though Mamma said that I would taste her hand if she ever caught me there. She even tried her stupid tales, saying that walking on graves was disrespectful and made the spirits angry, especially the spirit of Old May and the other old ladies. She said that there was an old man in the cemetery who went after young children to suck their blood like a *soucouyant*. But I had grown up listening to Mamma's stories. They didn't scare me.

But Mamma was popular; people even came to Mamma for medicine and advice because they said she had the sight. They asked about their future, their husbands, how many children they would have, or the boils on their skin.

I found Robin in the cemetery with the two Indian boys who worked for Mr Epps. Mr Epps told me that like all Indians they stole from him, but they made good curry for his *rotis*, so he kept them. I hailed Robin.

'Yeah, what?'

'I talked to Tambrun today,' I said, getting off my bike.

'Good one,' he said, chuckling. 'Real good one.'

I had to think of something for him to believe me.

'She asked me to have lunch with them next Sunday, I said.

'Yeah? You hear lie, that is lie. When I see you waving from A.C.'s verandah, I'll believe you.'

The two boys called out to him, 'You talking, or you playing?'

Robin ran back to the wicket, one of the boys bowled, and he hit a six across the graves.

When I got home that afternoon Mamma was washing over the sink and muttering something in patois. I tiptoed past the kitchen quietly and was about to open my door when she called me.

'*Veni ici, garçon*. Mr Epps told me you didn't do the messages for him this afternoon.'

Tambrun had made me completely forget about Mr Epps's errands. 'I went by the shop, Mamma, but Mr Epps wasn't there.'

Before I could finish, I felt Mamma's slipper on my back.

'*Salop!*' She struck me. "Don't lie to me, boy. And get out of this place before I go mad in here.'

I cursed her (in my head). Stupid bush woman couldn't even speak English properly, stupid small islander, stupid St Lucian. Sitting outside the house on the pavement, I stared at the Miller house for about an hour, wondering what Tambrun was doing inside and wondering how I was ever going to get onto her veranda.

The next morning I missed A.C. Miller's car because Mamma let me sleep late. That morning she came into my room carrying a cup of hot cocoa and fried bakes. I pretended to be still asleep so she tapped my back lightly. 'Wake up *dou-dou*, time for school.' Sometimes she could be like that and I was sorry I cursed her.

I had a week left and still no plan. In school I spent the twenty minutes of prayers before class thinking about A.C. Miller's verandah. The priests, especially Father Petri, were so proud of me since I concentrated so hard in my prayers. That week they even gave me the Honourable Student prize. 'Talking to the Lord is a serious matter, Mr Harris, and you have shown that you are a good Catholic.'

After school I usually took the shortcut through the cemetery to look for the boys. But that afternoon it was empty except for one little boy who was wetting the soles of his feet under the standpipe to cool them off from the hot pitch road. He told me no one had been there so I went to the Savannah. I sat under the tree close to where we usually played football and waited but they didn't show up there, either. This was our favourite spot around the Savannah because the bench was directly opposite The Queen's Royal College where both Robin and I wanted to go after we sat our eleven-plus exams. I could already see myself in the royal-blue shirt with the emblem on the pocket and the khaki shorts. I bought two glasses of oysters (the old men around the Savannah told Robin and me that oysters were good for our backs) and waited until late afternoon, hoping that Tambrun would come. A second group of men came to work the night shift on the coconut cart. It started to drizzle. Soon the rainy season would be here and the sick people would start coming to the house for Mamma's green water she made from rabbit bush. The smell would linger in our house until the dry season.

She wouldn't come today. So I rode around the Savannah one more time before going home. When I was only halfway down the Boulevard, I saw a crowd of people outside the Miller house. There was an ambulance van and a police car. The first people I saw there were Mr Epps's two Indian boys. I asked them what was going on, but they didn't say anything. Then I saw Robin sitting on top of his wall eating a *roti*. The way he looked, it could have been a cricket match.

'Tony, you miss all the action, boy!' he said.

I got off my bike and Robin jumped off the wall, tossing the *roti* paper into the gutter.

'They taking the aunt to the mad-people home. I hear she almost stabbed A.C.'

'And what about…?' But before I could finish, Robin contin-ued.

'The boss man all right, don't worry. But I not surprised. Ali was telling me that he kept her locked up.'

I shook my head. 'You always getting things wrong, Robin.'

'All right, just ask your girlfriend Tambrun, then,' he said.

The ambulance drove off, making a sound like a screaming old lady. People started going back to their houses on both sides of the street. Robin looked so happy, so excited, I wanted to wring his skinny neck, but Mamma saved him.

'Come inside, Tony!'

'Your Mamma calling you, boy,' said Robin.

When I went in, Mamma was peeping through the kitchen window.

'They took the old lady, Mamma.'

'I know, Tony.'

'You think A.C. Miller is a good man, Mamma?'

She turned to me and said, 'There are no good men after your father.'

I had heard this ever since my father died when I was seven.

'But I always say those houses across the street don't have enough light. It isn't right to keep people inside, even if your house big like the Savannah.'

I saw the rabbit bush in the sink; it made my stomach feel sick.

That night before I went to bed I thought about what Mamma and Robin had said. And I decided that it had to be from jealousy. Jealousy was the little green monster that fed on dirty hearts. Father Petri said that it could make you lie. And then I had a revelation, the perfect excuse for Robin. The house of Miller could never have guests at this time; it was a natural escape. So I closed my eyes and hoped to dream of another task. Crick-crack.

The Miller name got a rest from the old-aunt story after two French Creole families from the Boulevard got married. Mr Richard Montplaisir and his new bride were on the front page of the *Express* and *Evening News*. I cut out all their pictures and put them next to the article about the aunt, which had the heading 'Bacchanal on the Boulevard'. And everything was fine until a certain Chin family moved onto our side. Before long there were little Chinese boys running around handing people paper with 'Coming Soon Chin & Sons Laundermat' written on it. It bothered me because the French Creoles would tolerate a *roti* shop, but a whole laundermat was carrying the joke too far. Soon they would want our side of the street to leave! Maybe no one else saw it because they were too busy *fêting*, but I could feel it coming like I felt Mamma's hand before it reached my face.

And all this background was to fatten the middle, like Father Petri said. It was to explain what I had to do for Mamma, for me and for Tambrun too. I needed money for us all to leave the Boulevard when the time came. So Robin and I decided to borrow, only borrow, a little money from the Sacred Heart Church collection. And no one would have known if Robin hadn't proceeded to spend the money on a little *dougla* girl he was trying to impress. Right after Sunday Morning Mass he took the girl for boiled corn, coconut water and a 12.30 matinee. Mr Epps became suspicious; all Father Petri had to do was ask Robin a few questions and he betrayed me in a second.

So for a month Robin and I had to get up at five o'clock to help Father Petri set up the church for Mass. We had to say a Hail Mary for every dollar we borrowed. We said about fifty. The only thing that helped the punishment was a lady always dressed in red who passed my window every morning. I listened for the click-clack of her high heels hitting the pavement. Through the holes in my crochet curtain, I watched her dress sway from east to west like the pendulum of a clock. And then she would disappear until next Sunday. Sometimes I thought about her in church. But soon the laundermat idea would come back and I remembered Mamma and Tambrun.

Mamma would have to go back to St Lucia or live with my uncle in Toco. Tambrun and I, being city folk, would have to live in the north. Only two real problems remained. I hadn't actually spoken to Tambrun. The last time I saw her, she kept her head straight and stiff. The other problem was that I had no idea where I could take her. And she was used to the big house, plenty of food,

seven servants and a yard-boy like Ali. Before I went to bed
Mamma came into my room, carrying a cup of orange-peel tea.
She kissed my forehead and said, 'Remember *doux-doux*, you
have to help Mr Epps in the morning.' After she left, I said two
Hail Marys and made a list. Number one to talk to Tambrun,
number two, to find a way to talk to her.

I had two more Sundays in church with Father Petri. The red
lady's steps didn't wake me anymore, now it was just the sound
of rain that seemed to pierce holes in the roof like nails. There was
the sound of thunder and I would need a tent. Before going to
church, I passed the sign 'Coming Soon, Chin & Sons'. I didn't
have much time left. Even though I was late for church, I went up
to the racetrack. I rode on the grass and followed the jockeys until
they disappeared, going deeper into the Savannah where the trees
were thicker. I waited for them but they never came back.

That night there were stars. The *petit carême* season was here, so
the rains would stop for a while. I went into my room hoping to
find a way into the Miller house. Robin and his *dougla* girlfriend
hailed me outside my window. I turned off the light and sat on the
floor. I wanted to be alone; I was thinking. Mamma called me for
dinner. She had left a hot plate of *pelau* for me on the table. Across
the room Mamma sat in the chair my father had made for her. She
said that he kept the chair warm. But it was *petit carême* season
when my father died, and Mamma was missing him. 'Good night,
Mamma,' I said and kissed her forehead.

On some mornings, the sun could turn my room into an oven.
I woke up sweating. Mamma was standing over me with a bottle
of green water in one hand, a purse in the other.

'Your grandma's sick. All this sun, then rain, then sun again.
Stay with Mr Epps until I come back tomorrow evening.' She
kissed me and left.

And then I heard a little voice inside me say, Tony, it's time. A
little devil came into the house and into me. He made me go to
the kitchen and eat all the cold food in the pot. He made me turn

on the radio and sing all the old calypsos and dance around holding a bottle of water by the neck, pretending it was rum. I laughed loud and hard like the old men who played cards outside the College Pub. Then I stuffed my school bags with clothes, closed the door and left the little devil behind. Tambrun and I – I had decided – would leave that night.

I waited that night for Mr Epps to go to bed and for Robin and his girlfriend to leave. From Robin's wall I could see straight into the Miller house. All the lights were on inside and the yard was as bright as day. I stared across the street for a long time. I thought I saw the Red Lady calling me from the street, saying, Tony, it's time, but when I ran across, she vanished like a spirit.

I stood by the gate waiting for Felix to smell me, and when he didn't I went into the Miller yard. It looked like a small savannah. A.C. Miller's long black car was parked in the garage. I ran my hands along its cold body. Above the garage were the servants' quarters, where Mamma's friend lived. All over the garden were huge clay pots, big enough to hide seven men. Then again everything seemed bigger than normal, like a palace. At the side of the house, I found an old kerosene tin. I propped it close to the wall and stared straight into a bedroom.

Then she came into the room. My beautiful Tambrun! With the eyes like clear green Tobago water! I held my stomach because I felt I would burst from happiness. She stood in front of a long mirror and untied the bow in her thick brown hair. She raised her skirt just above her knees. For a second I thought I was in a dream, feeling so full inside. Tambrun tried to spin on one leg. She tried once, twice, and then suddenly the door opened. She froze before A.C. Miller.

'You should be getting ready for bed now, Nicky,' he said.

Tambrun looked down to the floor. Her eyes looked full and watery. 'Sorry, Uncle.'

A.C. walked over and patted her on the head. 'Be a little more thoughtful. Your aunt needs her rest now.' He walked to the door. 'I'll call Rose for you.'

In a few minutes Rose was in Tambrun's room. I wanted to

cover my mouth because I felt they could hear me breathe. I clutched the windowsill to keep my balance. Rose went over to the large wooden chest of drawers and took out a yellow night-gown; she spread it on the bed for Tambrun.

'Mr Miller say you have to go to bed now, Miss Nicole.'

Tambrun handed Rose a brush. She stroked Tambrun's hair gently. Then Rose helped her get her arms out of her blouse. I tried my best not to look but her skin was so smooth and brown, like the colour of honey with just a drop of milk. Tambrun turned and hugged Rose. 'Come with us, Rose,' she said, 'it's going to be so lonely.'

Rose just smiled. The night breeze blew through Tambrun's curtains and into her room.

'You'll catch a chill, Miss Nicky, with this open.'

Before Rose got to the window, I jumped off the kerosene tin, hitting it with my foot. Felix barked and I thought I saw the Red Lady in the yard. Ten *la diablesse* spirits were behind me so I ran, never looking back, until I got to Robin's room.

Robin was half asleep on his bed. 'Where you coming from at this hour, man?'

'I went out for some fresh air. The night so hot.'

Robin smiled in a strange way, then I smelt the stale alcohol lingering above his mouth like flies. He passed out. I couldn't fall asleep because all the lights were still on across the road in the Miller house. When I finally fell asleep, I had a nightmare that everyone on the Boulevard was chasing me, holding signs with 'Coming Soon, Chin & Sons' written on them. More than once, I had this dream, in between Robin's trips to the toilet.

The next morning, I left Mr Epps's house early before anyone was awake and I strayed into the street, feeling I had let my side of the street down. I was sure they would make us leave; it was like that for people like us, even though we were here first. Then I looked up for a second and saw her walking alone towards the Savannah. From the way Tambrun looked at me, I could tell she wanted me to cross the street.

'I remember you,' she said.

I remembered her changing in front of the mirror and I felt my face getting hot.

'It's rude to stare, you know,' she said.

'Sorry.'

'From now on,' she said, 'I'm going to walk around the Savannah every afternoon before we move to San Miguel. We have to move to San Miguel. My uncle is selling the house.'

San Miguel was a cocoa estate and soon there would be another boy looking at her, wanting to marry her. 'How can you leave the Boulevard?'

Just then, Rose came out of the gate.

'I have to go,' Tambrun said.

'Come inside for your breakfast, Miss Nicky.'

Tambrun nodded and they walked back into the house together.

A month later, the day after my grandmother died, Tambrun and the whole Miller family left for San Miguel.

They buried my grandmother in the cemetery close to us at the foot of the Boulevard. It was a hot, sunny day. Mamma had to hold onto my uncle's arm because she said her legs were weak. My uncle said that she took my father's death better, because the hardest thing is to lose a mother. Everyone on our side of the street came. Friends, Mr Epps, Robin, his girlfriend and all the people Mamma helped. And although none of them ever met Grandma, they said she was a good soul. That day, what Father Petri had said to us in school made sense. The end will come when it will come. So the day of the funeral I cried for Mamma. But to tell you the truth I cried because 'Chin & Sons' was open, the Miller house was empty and Tambrun had left for San Miguel.

Once upon a time, I lived on a street so wide it separated the two sides like the sea separates two islands, and on that street lived a girl with eyes as green as Tobago water, and one day I would make my way to the other side, crossing over if only to get a glimpse of her. Crick-crack.

THE LONGEST ROPE

The night before she left Andy, her husband of six years and father of one-year-old Lulu, Katharine Gill, née Howard, dreamt about her mother who had passed away a day before Katie's seventh birthday. In the dream her mother was reading from the huge red book with her favourite fairytales, the one she always read from to Katie before her afternoon nap. They lay facing the window in her parents' room on the same faded blue-and-white floral sheets her mother loved. The old room felt the way it used to, shady and cool, protected from the scorching after-lunch heat by the sprawling branches of the hog plum tree. Then suddenly the tiny brown head of a snake with a stick-thin body slithered across the covers. Katie sat up. 'Look, Mummy, look!' she said. Without saying a word, her mother got up, snatched the curling snake and tossed it out of the window like an old orange peel. They had begun to read again when a second snake slid in between them. Again her mother grabbed the snake and threw it away, but before she could lie down, the biggest of the three snakes raised an enormous head with shiny, black-marble eyes. The thick, long, oily body curved and spread over the blue flowers on the sheets. This time Katie had to help her mother lift the snake to the window. Katie was terrified of snakes; she couldn't even look at them when her parents used to take her to the zoo on Sunday afternoons, but because her mother seemed merely irritated by all that up and down, Katie felt safe. In the dream she never saw her mother's face but she knew it was her mother from her hands: the puffy fingers, the short, bleached nails and the muddy coloured skin with thick veins spreading like roots beneath the earth.

The next morning Katie related the entire dream to her housekeeper, Patricia, Head Mother of the Red Hill Spiritual Baptist, who cleaned homes by day and cleansed sins by night. She shook her head, then told Katie that snakes were enemies and these enemies lay close to her, but she would get rid of them and her mother would help her from the other world.

It was exactly three o'clock when Katie and John pulled up in front of Mr Willis's house on the top of the hill. The two-story white block with burglar-proofed windows and dark-grey iron doors made it look like a prison. A staircase built on the outside of the building divided the house in two. The postbox attached to the gate had no number, but John saw Mr Willis's Volkswagens and knew it was the house. He pulled up the handbrake and left the Jeep in gear so it wouldn't roll down the hill. They got out. A thick, iron chain wrapped loosely around the green gate barely held the two collapsing sides together.

'You go first,' Katie said to John, pushing him against the shaky gate.

'You're such a coward Howard,' he teased. 'Howard the Coward.'

Usually Katie would laugh at John's old joke, which he had used since high school. He always called her Howard even after she became Mrs Gill.

'Bad mood?' John nudged her.

'Yeah, very bad, you idiot.' She finally gave in and giggled.

During the day they still played their buddy role, teasing, flirting, the way they used to before Katie showed up at John's door at four o'clock one Sunday morning.

John removed the chain. The steep, narrow driveway was slippery from the moss growing in between the cracks in the concrete. Except for a shrivelled bougainvillea in a large white pot next to a patch of brown grass, the yard was bare. But in the middle of this desert, two Volkswagen bugs, one blue, one green, glistened like water in an oasis. Their silver fenders shone in the hot sun, their hoods reflected Katie's and John's faces like mirrors. Through the spotless windows, they peered inside these antiques and saw glossy, beige, plastic upholstery. The new model Volkswagen, the one Katie and John had come to see, was parked in the covered part of the driveway; it was a metallic green. They were about to examine its interior when Betty and Bonnie rushed out from underneath the stairs. Mr Willis's two half-starved, mangy, mongrel bitches had been hiding and waiting for their prey to get closer.

'Christ, what the hell!' John yelled. Katie screamed. They both pelted down the driveway and leapt into the Jeep with John shouting, 'WALK, DON'T RUN!' Betty and Bonnie barked, growled and circled the Jeep. John and Katie looked at each other and started to laugh.

'Who's the Coward now, Mr Walk Don't Run?'

'Good thing the gate was still open,' said John and they both cracked up again. He tooted the horn and inched down the window. 'Good Afternoon. Good Afternoon.'

Finally the master appeared at the top of the stairs. He was a small man, slight, sixtyish, with a short greying Afro and big square glasses. Although his red 'Coca Cola Is It' T-shirt was faded, he had neatly tucked it into his black sweat pants, which fell just above his bleached white socks and tennis shoes. Mr Willis trotted down the stairs to the gate.

'Betty, Bonnie, come here, naughty girls.' The voice matched the quiet, gentle one John had spoken to on the phone.

'So sorry, really sorry about that... I was listening to the cricket with the headphones on because the madam was taking a rest. I must have dozed off, I really don't like to make people wait, especially when you have come from so far.'

They hadn't really come from so far. John and Katie lived in the West, Mr Willis lived in the East; a highway got you in and out of the two worlds in thirty minutes, but if there was traffic it could take days – at least that was the joke. The most dangerous thing about the drive was the maxi-taxis farting thick, black smoke from their old diesel engines, blasting the latest Jamaican dub and packed with heads bobbing up and down. The maxis swerved in and out of the lanes, stopping suddenly on the highway to let out some heads and pile more in. John called them Kamikaze drivers. There seemed to be thousands of them on the road, particularly in the west where they brought in the housekeepers, the babysitters and the gardeners from the east to the richer neighbourhoods on the island.

Mr Willis kept apologizing but John assured him they hadn't been waiting long. Katie said nothing, just nodded in agreement. Betty and Bonnie were now pretending to be playful puppies for their master, burying their noses between his thin legs and flat bottom.

'Let me tie them. The other day, they rushed the mail lady and she dropped all of my mail in the gutter.' He finally managed to get a hold of their collars and dragged them to the bottom of the stairs where there were two rusty chains.

John and Katie got out of the Jeep and walked into the yard again when they were sure the dogs were tied. Mr Willis stood in the carport assuring them that 'the area was secure'. They all shook hands and introduced themselves; John, Katie and 'Harold Willis at your service'. John towered over the tiny Mr Willis, who was just about Katie's height but half her width.

'Well, this, I believe, is what you have come to see.' Mr Willis gently patted the hood of the car. John looked at the car again and muttered a few pleasant remarks. The Germans made the best cars in the world and Mr Willis was sure that this one, the Polo, would perform as well as her older relatives; he pointed to his precious bugs. They compared BMWs to Audis to Porsches, discussed American cars with Japanese engines, and Japanese cars with European designs. Katie quickly lost interest. She had already decided that she liked the car's body, its colour and the price. John would tell her whether or not it was a good deal. Katie was drawn to the lower half of Mr Willis's house; the huge space felt empty. There was burglar-proofing on the inside of the louvres but most of the glass slats were missing or cracked, leaving two sharp metal edges holding air. The crocheted curtains, probably once white, were now cream and sagging with dust. Katie peeped through the holes in the floral pattern. In the large, dimly lit room, she saw the shape of a stove, a fridge jammed against a wall and a long, thin cot in the middle of the floor with a pillow.

Mr Willis unlocked the car's doors with a knob on the key ring. The back seats were still covered in plastic even though the car was about six months old. He had bought 'her' because his boss had promised him a promotion. But now, instead of a promotion, Mr Willis faced early retirement. That was why he had to sell the car, which had been 'bought on the premise of a promise', a phrase Mr Willis loved to repeat. The madam had said that he was a fool to think he would get a promotion at his age. It was obvious to her that his boss just wanted to make sure he would keep working like a dog until his last days. Mr Willis said that he should have trusted the madam since she had always been so 'perspective'.

'But when God closes a window, he opens a door. That's what they say and I believe it too, even if the madam thinks I'm a fool. Anyway, enough of that, you are here about this little lady. I thought we could give her a good test if we went up to the Fort. Is that okay with you?'

John said that it was fine. 'Splendid,' said Mr Willis, excusing himself again as he jogged up the stairs into the house. Katie thought she saw a head covered with small pink-and-green curlers peeping through curtains upstairs. But before she could ask John if he had seen the head, Mr Willis reappeared sporting a black baseball cap with the New York Knicks stitched in red.

'The last time we went to New York, the madam and I took in a game at Madison Square Garden. You've been to New York I suppose… this was my first time, the madam's second, in fact it was her second time with her second husband.' Mr Willis gave a nervous tee-hee kind of laugh with a wide tight smile as though someone was pulling his cheeks from either side of his face. Katie looked at his dry, over-washed, cracked, brown skin that seemed to be covered with a film of white soap; he smelt like a bar of Lux.

Mr Willis opened the car door for Katie, insisting that she sit in front. Before he handed the keys over to John, he offered to take the car out of the driveway. 'Up to you,' John said, sounding certain that he didn't need any help at all. The plastic covering the back seat made a quiet, shrieking, stretched-plastic sound as Mr Willis sat down. Katie buckled herself in and noticed a small, white pouch filled with lavender-scented potpourri in the side-door pocket. Next to the small sack was a miniature, green cardboard Christmas tree that had an overpowering pine smell. Katie was now nauseous, adding to the already uncomfortable feeling she had because the skin of her flabby, post-Lulu stomach folded over her skirt.

She tortured herself because Lulu was a year old and she still had ten pounds to lose. Standing naked in front of her bathroom mirror, she tugged at her flesh, held in her stomach and imagined a younger body. During her unhappy pregnancy, she gained fifty pounds. Andy used to tease her with names like 'Elephant Woman', 'Katie the Cow' or 'Fatty Katty'. Sometimes she laughed it off and sometimes she cried, even though Andy was always 'just joking'. The dark-blue denim shirt she had borrowed from John covered her 'Lulu fat', but now she was incredibly hot. She wiped her damp forehead with a sleeve and tightened her ponytail.

As they got onto the main road, Mr Willis reminded John about their destination.

'You know how to get to the Fort... John, is it?'

'Yeah, been there a few times,' John said smiling. 'It used to be quite a romantic spot, until they started to rob you and beat you up.'

'Yes,' Mr Willis agreed, 'quite the romantic spot.' They both laughed like guilty teenage boys. Katie had been staring at the mats. There were two sets of them on the floor, the original mats that came with the car and then thicker, grey plastic ones over the first layer to protect the original ones from getting dirty. A white

cloth was folded neatly on the dashboard to wipe away any dust
that settled there.

The car bucked a couple of times. 'Getting used to the gears,'
John said, still very confident.

'Yes, it takes a little time, but soon you'll get the feel of her and
it'll be fine.' Mr Willis unbuckled his seat belt and leaned forward.
He seemed a little nervous.

Now almost a year old, Lulu never slept through the night, and
only for her first two weeks at home had she slept right through.
Since then, she always woke at two in the morning and again at
four. Katie nursed her for the first four months and then hoped
and prayed that a bottle and magic formula would buy her a
night's sleep. She always went to bed with the weary feeling that
very soon Lulu would wake up and the torture would start all over
again. At one point she wanted to bring Lulu into her bed, but
Andy's mother warned him about bad habits that were hard to
break and besides, his mother added, the child could even suffo-
cate. So Andy decided that Lulu would stay in her own room. He
never got up anyway, and if for some reason Katie didn't hear the
monitor, which was rare since Katie could feel that Lulu was
about to cry even before she whimpered, Andy would tap her and
say, 'She's up.' Andy didn't get up because Katie could take a nap
during the day while Lulu slept, and in fact, according to Andy,
Katie should consider herself lucky since some mothers had to
work in the day and get up at night to see about their babies.

The night Katie left Andy, Lulu had already gotten up three
times by two o'clock. Each time Katie put her back down gently
into the crib, the screaming would begin again. Katie had spent
most of the night back and forth to Lulu's room: picking her up,
putting her down, covering her, pulling down the net, tiptoeing
to her bedroom, getting under her covers, holding her breath and
waiting for the screams to start again, and they did. Andy never
moved. He lay there like a huge lump on the bed. Katie held Lulu,
patted her back, walked up and down the hallway, sat in the chair

next to Lulu's crib, rocked her back and forth, and sang her favourite lullaby, 'Doh doh petit popo, petit popo ka fait doh doh', over and over again. She covered Lulu with a blanket, took it off. She turned on the fan, she took it off, not sure if Lulu was too cold or too hot. The piercing scream continued so Katie hummed a little louder and patted Lulu's back a little harder. Katie paced back and forth from the living room to the dining room. Then she opened the front door and started to walk Lulu outside in the dark.

The ground was cold and damp, the grass wet from the early morning drizzle. Katie was now crying too, pressing Lulu close to her body, squeezing her, singing loudly and still no Andy in sight. Katie knew she could leave right now and he would just think she had finally gotten Lulu back to sleep and had decided to stay in the nursery. Her wallet was in the kitchen; her slippers were next to the couch. She was wearing her usual nighttime uniform, long tights and a big T-shirt. Lulu had on a long sleeper. Suddenly Katie grabbed her wallet, put on her slippers, pulled in the front door, closed the gate and walked up the street towards the main road, hoping to get a maxi-taxi at three o'clock in the morning.

It had begun to drizzle. A light rain fell in the bright sunlight, like grains of salt pouring from the sky. John fumbled around for the right knobs; the windows finally went up. He asked Mr Willis how to turn on the air conditioning unit. Mr Willis hesitated then said, 'I never really drive her in the rain. I usually take the other car when I see rain over the hills. The potholes are like pools around here and all that mud underneath her... leaves her in such a mess.'

Despite all his fears, he managed to tell John how to put on the AC unit. Katie didn't know which was worse, the warm rain or the cool air that trapped in the sickly smells of the lavender potpourri and pine. She tugged at the waist of her skirt hoping John wouldn't notice. He had always been lean and muscular with the body of a swimmer. Still trying hard to look like an American graduate student, John usually wore a pair of faded

Levis and a white T-shirt. His almond brown hair was shiny and dead straight. 'Hair that girls would kill for,' Katie would say. He wore it long and a little messy over his eyes. His skin was fair enough for him to get comments like, 'White Boy' or 'Move Your White Boy Tail' or 'Haul Your White Boy Ass' from his friends, even though John thought he looked as brown as the rest of them.

When they were just married, before Lulu was born, Katie and Andy usually went out on Saturday nights to one of Andy's friend's homes for dinner. She dressed for these dreaded dinners in high-heeled sandals and what Andy called her 'fuck-me' dresses. Most of the women in the room shopped at the boutique where Katie used to work; they seldom spent more than twenty minutes in the store but in that time they could easily spend Katie's monthly salary on a dress.

Everyone in the room except Katie had studied abroad. They could all tell jokes about undergraduate years in Boston, London and Washington. They could compare Chinese restaurants in New York or Indian restaurants in London. They could talk about museums in Paris and parties in Spain. So as the plates were being cleared for dessert served with coffee, tea or more wine, Katie would move away from the arguing, laughing table that spoke this foreign language. She would hide behind a magazine or a book she wasn't really reading until Andy was ready to leave.

Mr Willis was beginning to relax. He finally sat back. The gears were going in smoothly, John was handling her well.

'You know some people, especially the ladies, prefer the automatic, but I must confess I am a stick-shift man, like yourself, I see.'

'Yes, I never really had an automatic,' John said, talking into the rear-view mirror, 'but this purchase is actually for the lady.

Mr Willis apologized, he was embarrassed, had forgotten his manners, had said very little to the lady and was very, very sorry.

Katie didn't say anything. She was thinking about Lulu. Although they had only left her for about an hour, she was worried that Lulu would miss her mama and start to cry. Katie seldom left Lulu alone, even with Andy. During the first month of her life, Andy dropped Lulu while he was trying to give her a bath in the sink. She squirmed, slipped from his hands, hit her head against the tap, and pink water flowed down the drain. The sight of blood on her baby girl terrified Katie. She grabbed Lulu, swore at Andy and examined the small incision. Andy accused her of overreacting, picked up his car keys and left Katie alone with Lulu for the rest of that Sunday.

As Katie reached the main road on the night she left Andy Gill, she stood under a streetlight. The valley was cool with a starlit sky. Katie had never seen so many stars. The blackened hills looked as thin as cardboard against this Christmas-tree night so she tried to think about the smooth, round, sparkling heavens instead of the empty street and the baby she held. There was no one else around. Everything was quiet except for the occasional bark of a neighbour's dog. She rubbed Lulu's back; she had finally fallen asleep, resting her head on Katie's shoulder, touching the back of Katie's neck with her tiny fingers. Mosquitoes swarmed around their heads. Katie shooed them away with her wallet, trying her best not to wake Lulu.

A car drove by with two men inside; they slowed down just as they passed Katie and Lulu. One of the men turned around. Katie kept looking straight ahead of her. Then the car pulled off again. She hoped they had seen Lulu; a woman with a baby would be too much trouble for them. 3.30. She didn't know if she should walk further up the road, closer to the highway or wait there under the streetlight. Everything had become still: no wind, no cars, just the long, black, empty road with shiny dots where the streetlights hit the pitch. She kept looking in the direction of the taxi she needed, willing one to come down the street. 3.45. Katie started to walk towards the highway. Her arms and back were beginning to ache. She let her free arm hang for a moment before shifting Lulu to the other shoulder.

★

'I think you'll be happy with this vehicle, Miss, it's a car you can trust,' Mr Willis said.

John looked across at Katie, willing her to speak.

'Yes, I'm sure,' Katie said.

Mr Willis didn't seem to mind that she wasn't really listening to him.

'Trust is a funny thing,' Mr Willis said. 'The madam says that I am too trusting and so people take advantage of me. She calls me a doormat, a soft, silly, foolish man. But I told her that that is how I am. I trust. I believe in the good, even though I know that bad or even evil exists. I believe that things always work out in the end… Take for instance this car, I didn't think… Go straight, you can't go that way. It's a dead end…'

They started to climb the hill to the Fort. John swung around the first bend but had to stop suddenly to avoid hitting an old, white, rusty pick-up parked on the narrow road.

'You have to take it easy going up here, these people think they own the hill,' Mr Willis cautioned.

John realized that he would have to crawl up the hill to keep Mr Willis comfortable. He drove slowly around each bend. Mr Willis reminded him that he could always blow the horn if he felt he needed to. So from then on, John started to blow the horn for the blind turns. Katie hadn't been to the Fort in a long time. She was trying to remember whether she had been there since she married Andy. Before her father left for Miami with his new, young wife Wendy, he took Katie for a drive to the Fort. For a long time he had kept his vow 'to never marry again' and carefully hid any lovers he had from Katie. But two days before Katie's wedding, he presented Wendy to Katie like a gift he wasn't sure the bride-to-be would like. The two women couldn't trust each other at first; Katie wanted to remain loyal to a fading memory of her mother and Wendy wanted to show Katie's father what a good mother she could be. But as the years passed, the two women slowly put down their shields, allowing the tortured father and husband a little peace.

The steep, narrow road to the Fort had no name. At the bottom of the hill there was a sign written by a private citizen that said in fancy, flowery lettering, *Historical Sight.* John pointed the sign out to Katie and they both giggled.

'Now that's what I like to see; my own people taking the initiative!' said Mr Willis proudly.

Most people called it 'Fort Road' or 'The Hill'. There was a squatter settlement at the foot of the hill. The luckier families made homes of cracked, red-clay bricks but others had to settle for walls of rotting galvanize and discarded cardboard. A smell of dead dogs and faeces hovered above the settlement. Some bare-bottomed children wearing torn, buttonless shirts wandered around the dirt yards and played near the thick, black slush in the drains. As the road got narrower and steeper, the houses disappeared and trees with cattail vines, bamboo and tall razor grass reclaimed the hill. One or two families built their houses on the side of the hill that dropped into the valley; thin wooden poles buried deep into the ground held up the shaky, wooden boxes.

'The madam was telling me that although in this country the poor often have the best views, in Jamaica, where she lived for a little while with her first husband, the rich people live on the hills with the wonderful views.'

John made an umm, then swerved and stopped suddenly as he turned around the sharp bend. A thin, black girl holding a baby and a white plastic bag was crossing the road. She stopped, glared at John, cussed him and continued to cross. Her pretty, round face was many shades lighter than her body because of the pale powder she had caked onto her blue-black skin. A schoolgirl's plait stuck out and curled like a pig's tail. The made-up face looked no older than fifteen and her body had that awkward, disproportionate look of an adolescent with the dangling arms, spindly legs, and too-short torso. Her tight, red, spandex skirt barely stretched over a full-moon bottom; the mango-coloured halter left most of her tiny breasts and stomach exposed. But she had covered her baby from head to toe with a pink knitted woollen cap, long pyjamas and pink woollen booties. The girl's thin, baby-oiled legs made quick, click-clack steps in black high heels into a cave with a door called 'Hole in the Hill Bar and Guest House'. She disappeared inside with the baby.

Mr Willis and John had seen the girl but they both said nothing. Katie kept thinking about the baby in that dark, hot place. Katie hoped that once the mother got inside she would take off the cap and booties and give the baby a bottle of cool water.

The higher they climbed, the more poui trees they saw on the hillside and in the valley below. One or two trees grew on the side of the road and the flowers left a bright yellow carpet on the ground. It was very muggy now and the sun was shining again as light rain fell.

'I'm sure you know what they say when we have weather like this? The Devil and his wife are fighting.' Mr Willis gave a quiet laugh that sounded as if he was clearing his throat. 'Poui trees are a sign that we are definitely in the dry season, but we still seem to get rain every day.'

John said that he had noticed the trees as well. They talked about the change in weather all over the world, Global Warming and the Greenhouse Effect, even though Mr Willis kept talking about 'Global Warning' and the 'Green Peace Effect'. John didn't correct him. He understood what Mr Willis was trying to say.

Katie and John had talked about the pouis when they took Lulu to the beach the weekend before. Sitting on the damp sand close to the water, they could see the trees' bright, yellow patches on the hills that hugged the bay. Katie filled a bucket of sand with Lulu and tried her best to sound calm when she told John she wanted to find a job, a car and an apartment. John knew Katie well enough to realize that she was really asking if she could continue to stay with him. So he insisted that she stay in his apartment but he would help her find a job and a car. She also spoke to her father and Wendy later that evening, finally admitting to them that this was not just a short separation. Wendy understood; she had never been very fond of Andy, unlike Katie's father who kept telling her that sometimes men act this way, assuming that Andy had committed some 'indiscretion' and would soon 'get back on track'. He offered to send her some US currency and two tickets to Miami for a little vacation. 'Maybe later in the year,' was all Katie could say. Andy would always be 'a good guy' to her father. Her girlfriends used to tell her the same thing. She was lucky. Andy was a good catch. Good family. Good money. Good looking. He didn't stay out drinking with the boys on a Friday night, he paid all the bills, he cooked lunch on a Saturday, he made love to her on a Sunday night 'to start the week off right', and he adored his 'little Lulu'.

'I see myself like the tortoise,' said Mr Willis. 'I'm sure you know the story about the hare and tortoise. Well, tell me who wins the race? Take your time and you'll still get what you want in the end. I mean you'll still finish… fifteen years, imagine that, fifteen years and the madam says they were boring. I'm boring because I won't take risks like my fellow workers. They don't take risks, I told her, they take bribes. Yes, she says, and you are the only honest fool in that place. Yes, I am a fool, an honest fool, but at least I can close my eyes at night and not worry about facing the next day.'

'Not a lot of honest people left in this country.' John was ready to begin his lecture on crime, the government and the lack of punishment in the country. Katie had heard it before and Mr Willis just gave a slight 'huh' to be polite. He wanted to indicate agreement without implicating himself, lest some government informer in a passing car should overhear their conversation.

★

At nineteen, Katie believed she was as in love when she married twenty-five-year-old Andrew Gill. She imagined a very comfortable life, never worrying about money the way her father did on his civil-servant salary, never making lists to trace where every penny was going, never saying no when a daughter asked for a new pair of jeans for a school Bazaar. She envisioned a life filled with yes instead of 'It's been a hard month, sweetheart'. Every month was a hard month. In high school, when she pulled up to the school gate in her father's rusting, clanking, white wagon, her girlfriends would cover their mouths, whisper secrets and giggle. When she was out of the hot, smoky car, one friend would say to her, 'Your hair smells funky' or, 'When is your dad going to get a new car?' She would just smile and swallow away the familiar pain in her throat. After school, her father always arrived just after the bell so all the uniforms pouring out of the gate saw her get into the old car again. He knew she was embarrassed and sometimes he tried to give his Katharine the black shoes with the bow and the gold chain with the special heart links, but that would mean one bill left unpaid.

After high school, Katie began working in a boutique in the mall. Although she usually did well in her exams, she never tried to get the grades for the local University, even though her father promised he would 'find a way to pay for it'. Katie knew better. They owned nothing: there was no house to mortgage, no land to sell, no rich relatives to ask for help; the only thing they owned was that noisy, ugly car. One afternoon John introduced her to Andrew Gill. The next day and for the next two weeks Andrew appeared at the boutique and took Katie to lunch. She thought she was in love even before she discovered that Andrew's father owned the mall where she worked and two more in the south of the island. The courtship was short, the wedding (paid for by the groom's family) was grand. Their first two years of marriage had some peaks but after that it was mostly valleys. Mrs Gill treated Katie differently from her other daughter-in-law, but Katie made a point of not caring; she didn't have her father's life, she wasn't always broke, always worried, always wishing the month away to get the next pay slip. For almost all of the six years, Katie tried to make none of it matter.

'I am a man of my word, she's yours if you want her, Miss, but you must let me know by tomorrow because there is another young lady interested in the vehicle. All she needs is an okay from the bank for her loan. So I must tell you that although she was here first, I am inclined to give a nice young couple like yourselves the car. Are there any young ones, if you don't mind my asking?'

'Yes,' Katie said, 'a little girl.' She was willing to play the game if it was going to get her the car.

'Well I think that this lady would suit you well. She's very reliable.' He was leaning forward and talking through the space in between the front seats.

John avoided a tired, mangy dog slowly crossing the road. They were almost at the top now and the narrowing, winding road could barely hold two cars.

'And she's getting a good run today,' said Mr Willis, still leaning forward.

Two brick columns framed the entrance to the Fort with an empty guard booth on one side. 'An unmanned Fort,' Mr Willis said and chuckled. John drove in and parked next to the colonial-style main house that was once a museum. Katie remembered visiting the museum with her history teacher in high school; they had to write an essay about 'Spanish Colonization in the West Indies'. She sprinkled the essay with lots of Spanish expressions and called the capital Puerto de España instead of Port-of-Spain. She got an A for her efforts and left her paper lying around her desk for the other girls to see. B+s were rare in her high school, A's were almost extinct. Katie's British-educated principal, Miss Blackman, would always 'insist on excellence' since the English examiners, who still marked their Advanced Level examinations, were going to be extra hard on their ex-colonies.

They walked along a veranda that wrapped around the main house. Through the dirty glass on the French doors, they noticed that the large room was emptied of all the glass cases that once held dusty pieces of rocks, cannon balls and miniature models of English, Spanish and French galleons.

'This used to be one of my favourite places,' Mr Willis confessed. 'You could bring a young lady up here, show her the view and visit the museum. It used to be so nice.'

John picked up a couple of discarded Kentucky Fried Chicken boxes on the weedy uncut grass and placed them at the top of an overflowing bin. Quite a few young ladies had also accompanied John to the Fort, usually after a night of pubbing and partying, but the only thing the young lady saw was the back of John's father's wagon.

'A lady of few words,' Mr Willis said.

Katie smiled, trying hard to mask her irritation at this talkative little man.

'You look as though you have a lot on your mind, Miss, if you don't mind my saying so. But you know what they say…'

'No, Mr Willis, what do they say?' Katie wasn't trying to hide her feelings now, but Mr Willis just went on as though she had politely asked him to tell her.

'In local parlance they say, "The longest rope have a end." You know what that means, of course?'

John tuned in to smooth everything out, 'Exactly, that's what I always tell her… she worries too much, things always work out.'

Katie said nothing and just looked at the view; even John irritated her now. Things had certainly worked out for John. The night she arrived at his house with Lulu, she hoped he was alone so she could cry on his shoulder, get into bed with him and make him remember he had always loved her. She asked the maxi-taxi driver to drop her at John's front door instead of the main road. The driver, an old Indian man, didn't charge her any money at all and even opened the door for Katie and Lulu to get out of his little bus. Katie thanked him again and again, then walked to John's gate and pressed the buzzer. John's two Dobermans barked from the porch where they usually slept. A light was turned on. John stood in the doorway. He was alone and led her inside. No questions asked. They put Lulu in the guest bedroom on a blanket with a fort of pillows around her. John made coffee. Katie cried. John held her, kissed her on her cheek and she lifted her face so he could kiss her mouth. Then he took her into his bedroom and she lay down on the bed while he undressed her.

Mr Willis walked over to an old cannon whose barrel was

covered with brown crusts of rust like giant scabs. From the edge of the cliff he located Port-of-Spain's tallest buildings, the new highway and a cruise ship docked at the wharf.

John walked over to the edge of the grounds where Mr Willis stood and told him they had to get back.

'Sorry, I didn't mean to keep you; so nice and quiet here you know… never realized that I missed it,' Mr Willis said.

On the drive down the hill Katie asked Mr Willis a few questions about the car. She felt sorry about the way she had spoken to him earlier. He answered each question in his soft, polite way. They talked about the weather. A hot four o'clock sun was beating down on everything: the car, the black pitch roads and Katie's face. John drove cautiously; there were some maxi-taxis on the hill now. Work was finished for the day and people were going home to their shaky houses. When they passed 'Hole in the Hill', Katie glanced inside. The door was open and distorted calypso music blasted out of the black hole. A few fat-bellied taxi drivers had parked their vans at the side of the road and stood at the entrance sucking cold beers and shouting over the music. Some schoolboys, still in uniform, had strategically positioned themselves near enough to the road to catch a taxi heading up the hill and still have a clear view of the girls going into the bar.

For the rest of the drive back to Mr Willis's house, no one spoke. John followed the two suggestions made by Mr Willis on how to avoid the four o'clock traffic. But that was all they said until they pulled up in front of the gate.

'You can leave her outside,' Mr Willis said. 'With the other two cars in the yard the parking can get a little tricky.'

They all got out. Mr Willis shook their hands and thanked them again for taking the time to come and look at the car. He promised to call the next day but reminded them that he was a man of his word; the car was Katie's if he didn't hear from the bank-loan lady. Betty and Bonnie came down to the gate; this time they didn't bark. Katie felt as though someone was staring at them. She looked up to see the familiar head of pink-and-green curlers pop in and out of the doorway upstairs. Mr Willis saw her too.

'The madam must be getting ready to go out. She works 'til midnight almost every night now, selling her herbal products at her shop.' He took off his Knicks cap and massaged his temples; his puffy Afro held the cap's shape. Katie looked at him; his face suddenly appeared old and tired. 'Take care, thanks for taking the time to come all this way,' he said, but his quiet voice lacked its 'hope for the best' pep. John and Katie got into the Jeep, waved goodbye and drove off. When Katie looked back, Mr Willis was still standing outside his gate, staring at the ground.

Katie woke up early the next morning. It was still dark outside. She thought she heard Lulu crying but she wasn't. John was still asleep, making his bubbly, gargling sound. Katie had had another dream. This time she was bathing naked with Lulu in a urine-coloured river. Two men stood on the bridge above, staring at them. Lulu looked like nine or ten in the dream; she was holding on to Katie's waist whimpering. Then the scene changed and now their wet naked bodies huddled together in the back seat of a car. They were driving around Port-of-Spain at night with the same two men on the bridge. The streets had no other cars, only streams of people walking on the pavement and in the middle of the road. As she got closer, she realized it was a Carnival band of glistening bodies. They passed mothers giving piggybacks to tired, young masqueraders, sweaty drunk men play-fighting with fake swords, and teenage boys covered with blue paint and black grease, playing blue-devils with horns and tails, taunting the fighting drunks with their forked standards. The bodies touched and pressed against the slow-moving car but no one seemed to notice Katie and Lulu with the two strange men. Then Katie saw a tall, thin lady in a long-sleeved black dress standing next to a giant yellow poui tree in the middle of the road. Katie begged the men to stop. She was sure it was her mother. The men kept driving. Katie told the men she had to take Lulu home. But the two heads in front didn't look back and didn't say a word; they just kept driving through the streets and Katie knew she was going further and further away from her home.

She couldn't fall asleep again. It was five o'clock. She got out of John's king-sized bed. He mumbled something and turned over. In the kitchen, she put the kettle on the burner, took two mugs, measured the spoonfuls of coffee and sugar, and the drops of milk. She used to do the same thing every morning for Andy. As she sat at John's kitchen table, she began to make a list in her head: call Patricia about the dream, call Mr Willis about the car, and then there was the dry cleaning to be collected.

PINE HILL

Heather's Story

Heather dreamt of mornings like these when she used to feel like a fraud in a winter coat, freezing in some tunnel underneath Montreal; mornings like these in January, when the island light sharpened edges, unclouded colours, washed away muddy olive greens, changing them to a fresh lime, as fresh as this New Year's breeze on her face.

They were walking the route the Sunday before the famous Pine Hill Race. Simon, Heather's husband, had done the trail many times on his bike and had even come second in the race last year, losing out to young Hakim. But this year he wanted to walk the route, get a feel for it off his bike. Part of the stony track was just wide enough for his jeep to climb halfway up the hill but Simon wanted to walk all the way. And Heather was tired – no, exhausted. She hadn't had a straight six-hours sleep in months, ever since Phoebe was born, and since then Simon and Heather quarrelled even more than before. So Heather hoped Simon would see the effort she was making and hoped that maybe their luck would start to change. Recently she had become obsessed with change: rainy season to dry, Christmas to Carnival, Carnival to Lent, changes in her face, or even Phoebe's smile. But most of all, Heather was looking for a change in Simon.

As they began to walk up the first incline, Heather stopped to look at the next valley through a space that had opened between the trees. A powerful citrus smell came from the hill just behind her; she looked up to see terraces of orange, grapefruit, lime and pomerac trees. There was another tree she didn't recognize; its leaves were as broad as a breadfruit leaf but curled like fists, the way dry *bois canoe* leaves look when they drop to the ground. Heavy, pimply, reddish-brown balls dragged the tree's branches down. Some of its fruit had already splattered, revealing a bloody, fleshy pulp like ripe pomegranates. The smell was even stranger than the fruit, a sweet perfume that blended grapefruit with ylang-ylang and jasmine. An experiment for export, Heather imagined, started by the government and then forgotten. Heather wanted to pick it up and taste it. But Simon wanted to keep going, irritated that she was already lagging behind. Before long she was almost jogging, trying to keep up with him and at the same time appreciate the early morning sunlight blazing in between the hills of the next valley.

Tall fichus trees lined both sides of the trail, the branches interlacing to form a canopy over their heads. The path narrowed and blocked out most of the light. It was cool and shady now, with just a few rays of sunlight filtering through the spaces in the branches up above, freckling the damp ground. Fallen leaves and dewy grass made the path very slippery. 'Come on!' he yelled back at her. Once in a while a thick log lay across the route. Heather took a giant step, resting her hand on the mossy trunk, trying her best not to slide and fall. When she finally caught up with him, he was standing next to another log, waiting for her and glancing at his watch.

Simon had spent most of the weekend in his study after losing the race last year. He even refused to go to a business partner's wedding because he knew the Hakim clan would be there and young Hakim would sit and gloat for the entire afternoon. When Simon was in one of his moods, Phoebe couldn't fuss and all phone calls had to be short. But Heather had so few calls now that it didn't really matter; her girlfriends never liked Simon, and the one or two who stayed friendly with her had been insulted so many times by Simon they seldom called the house. Heather only saw them when they met for lunch every couple of months in unpopular places, and she hoped that Simon would never find out about it.

Looking at him now in his neat, belted, khaki shorts, olive polo shirt and clean white running shoes she knew he was thinking about the course, not them. But talking about change was useless. Heather saw their life divided into bills, Phoebe's doctor's appointments and grocery money.

'This is where I can make up a lot of time and pass that young fool.' 'This' was a long flat area that was dark, slippery and very narrow. They could barely walk side by side for the steep drop down. 'Hakim has no balls, just youth.' Then he laughed and Heather laughed too, even though he had said it a million times before.

Marriage is sacrifice, Heather's mother used to say. Her parents stayed married all their lives; their marriage survived a house fire, two miscarriages and her father's ten-year affair with a Swedish widow who lived down the street. Two months before she married Simon, Heather's father passed away. He had been very ill, and to be honest his death was a relief to her. Heather's mother was very strong and stoical at first; then one day she suddenly took to bed complaining of 'hellish migraines'. She wore grey on Heather's wedding day. One year later, almost to the day of Simon and Heather's first wedding anniversary, Heather was burying her mother. And once again she had to mourn rather than celebrate her marriage to Simon. Unfortunately, in those days, she wasn't looking for signs. Her father left her property and discipline; her mother, jewellery and sacrifice. That word 'sacrifice' always led to her mother's litany of sacrifices, everything she had given up to take care of Heather and her father: her acting, her dancing and her teaching. Her mother expected Heather to make similar choices, even though she never let her forget the sacrifices they had made to pay for Heather's expensive Canadian degree in English Literature. She tried to talk to her mother in the beginning about the awful fights with Simon, but her mother would often cut her off with 'The first few years are always the hardest' and, of course, 'Marriage is sacrifice.' Heather never really expected her mother to share her experiences with her; they were never close and her mother was not a particularly affectionate person. Heather felt that her mother resented how much attention and affection she received from her father. Her mother was a country girl, who grew up in Arouca, and became Dr Hart's wife, and maybe that was enough.

Simon was way ahead; Heather could barely see his shirt. Soon he disappeared and suddenly an incredible weight lifted and she didn't feel as though she was being dragged to the ground like that strange fruit. She could take her time and explore another path that led away from the course he expected her to follow. It was different from the others; she walked underneath tall, elegant bamboo whose branches crossed over her head like beams in a cathedral; the ground was covered with the bamboo's spiky brown leaves. She turned towards a steep, rocky incline and through some dense brush to a clearing full of tall nutmeg trees. Although the air felt damp, the sun lit the areas not shaded by the nutmeg branches, changing the green ground-cover to gold. From the first clearing she could see another terrace of more nutmeg trees. Before she made her way up to the second terrace she walked over to a trickling waterfall above a shallow pool of water. Cupping her hands she drank and splashed the ice-cold water over her face. Then she climbed up to the second terrace and stood in the middle of the tall, thin nutmeg trunks. Nutmegs covered the ground and a scent of spice and earth filled the air. She picked up a few of the dark-brown seeds wrapped in red leathery strands and put them in the side pocket of her cargo pants. As she reached into her pockets she found a clip, so she twisted her hair into a loose bun; Simon preferred her hair down, it didn't matter how hot she was.

Suddenly, male voices came from the track below. Heather froze, not knowing whether she should call out to Simon or not. The voices kept getting closer. She cowered behind one of the tree trunks, waiting, trying to breathe slowly, trying very hard not to scream. Then the voices faded and she waited a few minutes before venturing down the rocky slope. She felt foolish to have wandered so far away from Simon. Everyday there were reports

of another murder, another robbery, a rumour of a rape, and
Simon's daily reminders of how dangerous it was, living on this
'piece of rock, full of illiterate bandits who want what we have
without the hard work'. Simon thought they should get guns like
his Jamaican business partners and 'shoot their ass' when they
broke into their homes. Then she heard that voice that never left
her head.

'Heather! Heather!' He sounded angry, frantic. She went
down towards him. Once again on the track, she could almost
touch his back. Just as she was about to tap his shoulder, he flung
around, flailing his arms as though trying to stave off an attack.

'What the hell are you doing? Where did you go? Christ! How
many times do I have to tell you what could happen to you? You'll
understand when you end up like Mary, with a set of nasty bandits
spreading crap all over you after they've buggered you a thousand
times.'

He pointed his finger at Heather the way he always did when
he got into one of his rages. All she could do not to fall apart was
to fold her arms and bite the side of her mouth. He was still
ranting, even after they started to walk the track again.

'And now my time is totally screwed. Why did you come with
me if you knew you were going to wander off and screw up
everything?'

The yelling only stopped when they got to an open field where
a few cows and goats were grazing. Simon was right; Heather
knew she shouldn't have come. She asked him, he never asked
her. She was even surprised when he agreed. And her motives
were not purely charitable. Yes, she wanted to show support, but
she also wanted to see whether all those weekend rides were real
or whether she was being fooled like her mother, who only found
out about her father's affair while clearing away old papers in her
father's study. Then those voices she had heard suddenly came
back to her. She wanted to ask Simon if he had seen anyone else
on the trail but she was afraid he might use that information
against her in some way.

Beyond the field they climbed up another incline, razor grass reaching her waist, but Simon never looked back to check on her. Then he stopped, turned and said, 'This is the most difficult part of the race, this is Pine Hill.'

They both stood at the top with so sudden and steep a drop that Heather felt like stooping. The pine trees that grew on the slope looked as though they had been planted in straight lines. 'That's what makes it so hard,' Simon said. 'The trees are really scattered so it's hard to pick a line.' On either side of the hill, there was a quick plunge, one to a shallow rocky riverbed, the other to thorny brush and razor grass. Pine cones and spiky pine needles covered the ground making it 'difficult to negotiate, not to mention all those bumps,' he said, pointing to the ground which looked to Heather like her mother's hand, brown and smooth, covering a thick map of veins. 'Those hidden roots that run across the clearer areas are the real danger, especially when you start to pick up speed.' She walked at an angle, as instructed, down the treacherous hill, following Simon's lead. Halfway down she started to feel dizzy, so she stooped.

'What are you doing?' Simon shouted. He'd already gotten to the bottom. 'Just walk at an angle like I told you.'

Heather stood up for a moment and tried to take a step but the fear of falling over the side came back and she squatted again. Simon started yelling, but she didn't hear him anymore because she had started to cry, not her usual quiet cry but a loud bawl, like Phoebe when she was hungry or wanted to be picked up from her crib.

'Heather, come on, get up.' He didn't sound annoyed anymore and began to climb towards her, making his way up the hill by slipping on pine needles and grabbing hold of pine trunks. She wanted him to fall before he reached her. But he didn't. By the time he got to where she was squatting, her body was shaking.

'I'm tired, Simon,' Heather said, 'really tired.'

'What? Come on. Get up. I'll help you down.'

He held her around her waist. It was the first time he had held her in months. They slipped and skidded until they made it to the bottom of the hill. Then she pulled away from Simon and sat on a rock near the river. Suddenly, she heard the voices again. Simon moved closer to her. They looked up and saw three tall black shadows at the top of Pine Hill. The teenage boys were laughing and taunting each other until one of the boys, goaded on by the other two, began to make his wobbly descent. Quickly but tentatively as he began to pick up speed, he swerved just slightly to avoid a trunk but he lost control of his bike, flew over the handlebar and landed with a hard thump in the shallow riverbed near to where Heather was sitting. Simon let out a short snorting laugh. The two boys at the top of the hill who were jeering at first were now silent, rooted to the spot, stunned by the quick comic-strip fall. Then all at once they dropped their bikes and skated down the hill on their bottoms to get to their friend. Heather stood up and was about to go to the boy as well when Simon grabbed her arm and dragged her back down. As they were shielded by the tall blades of razor grass, the boys could have heard them but without seeing exactly where they were.

'We should help them and take the boy to the hospital or something. He looks really bad.' She pulled her arm away from Simon's grip.

'Shit! Keep bloody quiet or they'll hear us. We have to go now. I don't like how they look… It could be some ploy to rob us or something.'

'What ploy? The boy fell.'

'Shut up.'

He held her arm so firmly it hurt. On their way to the jeep, he kept her down low, stooping and peeping through the blades of grass. Of course he reminded Heather about Ronnie and Mary once again, saying that these days you couldn't trust anyone and those boys just didn't look right.

The boys called out over and over again, each time sounding more and more frantic. One boy even stood up, looked around, trying his best to figure out where the voices were coming from. There was panic and fright on his face, but Heather could clearly see there was nothing to say he was a bandit, as Simon wanted her to believe. The other boy remained hunched over the body that looked like one of Phoebe's unnaturally twisted Barbie Dolls. Heather and Simon stayed bent over until they got to their jeep. As they pulled away, they heard even more desperate shouts for help. They didn't stop until they got to the main road, Simon repeating all the while that the boys just didn't look right.

For the entire drive home, Heather didn't want to look at Simon, so she just stared out of the window, not really focusing on anything in particular. She felt for the nutmegs in her pocket. When she got home, she would crack them and grate the nut inside just to savour that smell of spiced earth once again. Nutmeg and cinnamon always reminded her of her mother's plaited tarts filled with the finest, imported apricot jam on the island. She never used the local guava jam even though Heather and her father loved it. She remembered the bright yellow apron her mother always put on, right after she carefully placed her diamond ring on a white saucer next to the sink.

That night, and every night for the entire week before the race, Heather kept looking out for something about the boy, on the news at night, or even in the newspapers. But there were no reports of any accident at Pine Hill. Simon had made her swear never to discuss what had happened with anyone and of course she didn't, at least until the Friday before the race. Heather decided to go to the Valley Plaza Pharmacy to buy medicine for Phoebe who had been suffering from a bad cold for a few days. The Hakim family owned the Pharmacy, so Simon never went there and expected that she would never shop there either. It was a small act of defiance but she felt as though it was the beginning of a change; at the Pharmacy she saw young Hakim and his brother strutting around and talking to their employees in a very gruff manner. The Pharmacy itself was extremely well-stocked and very pleasant. Heather decided that she would continue to shop there even though Simon was against it. But that feeling only lasted until she drove up the long driveway, when the thought of Simon bawling and screaming at her for going to the Pharmacy made her want to get rid of the Valley Plaza shopping bags as soon as possible. She called Miss Louise, her housekeeper, to help her take everything out of the car. It was only then, on seeing the bags, that Miss Louise told Heather about her son Trevor's recent job at the Valley Plaza Pharmacy. Miss Louise looked more worried than normal because she wasn't sure whether or not Trevor would keep the job since he hadn't been to work for a few days. All of this conversing was not typical of Miss Louise, who was always very quiet; she was an excellent cook and cleaner and took great care of Phoebe, but she seldom spoke or complained. She had worked for Heather and Simon since they bought the house in the valley three years ago, but they knew little about her life apart from the fact that she had a strong faith in her God and her church, and she had one son, Trevor, whom Heather had only met briefly. Heather sensed that some deep sadness had made Miss Louise this way and it would always prevent her from being truly free of whatever burden she carried. But while Heather unpacked the bags in the kitchen and threw them away in the garbage, Miss Louise began to tell her more about her son's fall off his bike, a bike she had gotten for him because he loved to ride; the fall had left him on crutches and she was afraid that the bike he so loved to ride would kill him.

'Where did he fall?' Heather asked, not expecting the reply.

'That place with all the trees, Pine Hill,' Miss Louise said.

Right at that moment Heather knew she should have confessed. But the shame was too great, so again she said nothing. But later that evening Heather told Simon what Miss Louise had told her. 'Imagine,' she said, 'we actually knew the boy.'

'Know what boy? We don't know that boy,' Simon said. 'How well do you know that boy? You don't even know Miss Louise's last name.' He sniggered because he knew it was true, she didn't know her last name. 'Look I don't want to go back over all that talk again. Just let it rest for Christ's sake.' And he walked away.

At the Pine Hill Race that Sunday there was a slight drizzle along with blazing sunshine; but the ground was wet enough to make the descent from the hill a little more difficult. Simon faltered slightly coming down although he managed to regain his balance, but it was just enough to let young Hakim pass him and take the hill as though he owned it, keeping his title of King of the Hill. Heather was anxious about how Simon would take the loss but this year he didn't seem to care as much. He just wanted to leave once the prize-giving ceremony was over; Simon only said that this would be his last race on the hill. And he was right; they never returned after that day.

Trevor's Story

Every morning, before he rode to work at the Valley Plaza Pharmacy, Trevor had to clean the yard, sweeping all the dead leaves under the sapodilla tree, scooping up the dogs' hard, stinking, black lumps with newspaper, then tossing it all over the wall into the swampy canal. Back inside, he drank a cup of warm cocoa, stuffed his knapsack with his Valley Plaza T-shirt and an old Flavor-Rite ice-cream container filled with the lunch his mother had cooked for him before she left for work at five in the morning, in the dark. By 6.30 Trevor was on his bike. Lately the climb over Sans Souci Hill only took half an hour; he had cut his time down by half since he started to work at the Pharmacy three months ago. These days Trevor dreamt about that early morning ride over the hill because the rains had finally stopped and the mornings were bright and windy.

On the climb up, if he was early enough, he usually passed Captain's ancient, house-and-land American car, packed with overstuffed school bags and screaming children in blue-and-white checkered uniforms. Captain, never without his sailor cap, dropped the children from the hill to Sans Souci RC, Trevor's old primary school. In the afternoon he would bring them back to his house and Mrs C would look after them until tired mothers collected tired children in the early evening. As he peddled alongside the house-and-land, Captain always gave Trevor a little *fatigue,* 'You ready for some early morning licks? I'll give you a head start?' Trevor replied, 'That old boat you driving there could never catch me, Grandpa.' Children's squeals and Captain's deep laugh flowed out of the giant automobile. Peddling up the hill was still hard for Trevor but the reward came at the top when he could fly down to the bottom. In the beginning he used to be afraid of the speed; once he started his descent, he would shift to a lower gear and pull on his left brakes. Now it was the opposite, he peddled faster just to feel that blast of wind on his face as he flew down.

Mr Hakim liked his employees in front of the Pharmacy by eight o'clock even though he opened the doors at nine. Usually they all sat outside on the steps, eating breakfasts of cold hops and sausage, bake and salt fish, or a doubles from 'Ali's Original Doubles' stand across the street. They washed the meal down with a cup of grapefruit juice or mauby from Mr Ali. At 8.45 Mr Hakim pulled up in his big, fat, silver Benz. His workers immediately stood at attention and cleared the steps to the entrance of the Pharmacy. The ones who still smelt of Ali's curry or salt fish stayed far away from their boss. A 'Good morning, Mr Hakim' chorus was greeted with a grunt. The doors unlocked, they all went quietly to their places: the girls in front set up the cash registers; the girls in the aisles made sure their shampoos and cosmetics were in order; Trevor and Gordon, the boys, went directly to the store room in the back.

Although they had been working together for months, they never discussed their jobs. Even while they sat on the steps in the morning, no one mentioned Mr Hakim or his sons, who had been accused of everything from robbery to rape but always walked out of the courts smiling. Maybe they felt that Mr Hakim's powers went beyond his bank account, so that he could hear them from his toilet seat, his breakfast table, or from the veranda of his mansion overlooking the Caribbean Sea. They never discussed the way Mr Hakim cussed them in front of customers, or how the Hakim brothers fondled the girls if they ever caught them alone in the bathroom. This Pharmacy paid more than most and they all said it was better than working in the cottage-cheese section in Mr Hakim's grocery.

They had seen Mr Hakim tear apart Sastri, a pretty aisle-girl, telling her to take her 'nasty, coolie cunt back to the country'. The girl crumbled in front of everyone and left the Pharmacy in tears that very morning, all of this because she kept asking an American lady to repeat what she was saying. Sastri couldn't understand the drawling, sprawling words. But America meant everything to Mr Hakim. He wanted the Pharmacy to look like the ones he had visited in New York, Washington and Miami. During their four-day training period, besides learning to pronounce the names of the American products (their instructor was Mr Hakim himself), they had to remember to always say, 'Have a nice day.'

All this information was lost on Trevor who only emerged from the storage room to carry more stock to the back. Only the pretty Indian and brown-skinned girls, hired by Matt and Mike Hakim, worked in the front with the two herculean, blue-black security guards from Tobago. The girls seldom spoke to Trevor, especially when the Hakim boys were around; then Trevor would become invisible, as invisible as he had been in his overcrowded high school. But he needed the little money thrown at him at the end of every month by Matt Hakim. Furthermore, Miss Jenny, Trevor's godmother, who was Mr Hakim's daughter's baby-sitter, begged Mr Hakim himself to give her godson a job. Mr Hakim had told her plain that 'those Negro boys only know how to thief, they don't want to know nothing about hard work.' But Miss Jenny promised that Trevor would work as hard as any Indian boy Mr Hakim could find. Then she promised Trevor, all two hundred and ten Grenadian pounds of her, to break his chicken neck if she ever found out he was playing the ass at the Pharmacy.

Through another friend, Miss Maple, a retired primary-school teacher also from Grenada, Trevor's mother, Miss Louise, found a tutor for her son. Mr Taylor lived just a few streets away from them in Sans Souci. After work Trevor could ride over the hill and be outside Mr Taylor's gate by five o'clock. Trevor had no difficulty finding the house for his first lesson. In a street where almost all the homes looked abandoned or recently hit by a hurricane, Mr Taylor's house was a blinding Clorox white. A

small doll's-house gate led into a narrow path painted red and
lined on either side with miniature yellow ixora in white concrete
pots that stopped abruptly at the front door. Trevor didn't notice
the buzzer the first afternoon and kept calling out 'Good evening,
good evening' from the road. Although Mr Taylor must have
heard Trevor from inside his doll's house, he refused to respond.
A passing neighbour, a middle-aged Rasta with greying locks
down his back, shouted to Trevor, 'Use the bell.'

The Rasta was right. The minute Trevor pressed the buzzer,
the door opened and a heavy molasses voice said, 'Come in.'
Inside, the house was so dark Trevor barely got a glance at the tall
shadow who told him to have a seat in the living room before the
figure disappeared again into the back room. The only light came
from a lamp with a yellow-and-red hibiscus print scarf draped
over its metal frame. The curtains in the tiny room were drawn,
the only pieces of furniture were two armchairs and a sofa covered
in thick, red velvet and a small, rectangular, thickly lacquered
mahogany table. An arrangement of plastic red roses in a white
ceramic vase had been carefully set on a crocheted doily in the
centre of the table. When Mr Taylor reappeared, he hovered over
Trevor like a giant. Trevor stood up. He looked closely at the
strange man; the hard, oily Brylcreamed, bottle-black hair was
combed forward over his face like a brush over a sharp cliff; the
purple forehead, stained from the hair dye, was lined and cracked,
covered with a layer of powder so it didn't shine like his polyester
baby-blue shirt or his shimmering, black, bell-bottomed pants or
even his gleaming black brogues.

Mr Taylor wanted to make good use of the hour and asked
Trevor to take a seat at the dining-room table. In two steps Trevor
was in the dining room. An old white bed-sheet was spread over
the polished table to prevent any 'unfortunate markings'. A green
copybook, a pencil and some sheets of paper were set before
Trevor. 'Excuse me,' he said and then disappeared yet again into
the black hole beyond the dining-room area. When he came back,
he was carrying a manila file and was smelling of Old Spice.

'We'll start with some poetry, Trevor, right? Yes, we'll begin with a little Yeats, an old friend who has kept me company many a lonely evening. You like poetry, young man?'

Trevor smiled and nodded but he felt extremely anxious. This Mr Taylor was costing him thirty dollars an hour, sixty dollars a week, two hundred and forty dollars a month, almost half of what Mr Hakim paid him. This time Trevor knew the English Exam syllabus by heart; he wasn't going to fail again. There was a multiple choice section on grammar and an essay about something general like 'The Environment', 'Violence on Television' or 'Globalization and the Banana Crisis in the Caribbean'. So he politely informed Mr Taylor that he had gotten the syllabus from the Ministry of Education, Culture, Gender and Youth Affairs, then pulled it from his knapsack and handed it to Mr Taylor. Trevor was sure he hadn't seen any poetry or anybody called Yeats.

'You repeating the exam, right, boy?' Mr Taylor's syrupy voice had disappeared.

'Yes, Sir.'

'So you want to repeat the same stupidness?'

'No, Sir, is just that I didn't see no poetry on the paper…'

'Double negative, my boy… There isn't any poetry on the paper and I do not care.' Mr Taylor was trying hard to regain his composure.

'You can't learn a language without its literature, my boy. In the old days you had to do both. You didn't have a choice, and tell me what we have now with all this choice! Now we have multiple-choice calypsonians: jump and wave, wave and jump, wine and wave; multiple-choice bandits: beat him, stab him, kill him; multiple-choice politicians: steal a little, steal plenty, steal enough. So just try your best to open that multiple-choice mind of yours.' Mr Taylor cleared his throat, 'Uh hum,' and in his best Sans Souci version of the Queen's English recited Yeats:

> When you are old and grey and full of sleep,
> And nodding by the fire, take down this book…

Trevor only heard a droning voice and words buzzing like flies in his ears. He could have put the same thirty dollars towards part of the hundred-dollar pre-registration fee for the Pine Hill Race, or even for a new seat cover for his bike. Only fifteen minutes had passed and already he felt as though he had made a mistake. Grammar. He needed grammar; when to use 'could' or 'can', 'would' or 'will'; he was never sure. Vocabulary and lists of words like 'endemic', 'empirical' and 'didactic' – words to make his essay sound impressive. He didn't want poetry, he wanted a pass. And without a pass in English, there would always be a Mr Hakim.

> And bending down beside the glowing bars,
> Murmur, a little sadly, how Love fled.

Mr Taylor kept talking about love and truth but Trevor could only think about the wasted money. By the end of the hour he was irritated, felt no closer to a pass, but promised to use the buzzer next time.

When he got home that evening it was nearly seven o'clock. He opened the gate to be greeted by all of his uncle's smelly pot hounds circling and snapping at each other. On the outside the two houses in the yard looked exactly alike but on the inside they were as different as his mother and his uncle. Dub music, Soca, cussing and children's shrieks filled his Uncle Patrick's house, while his sister, Louise, had a clean, still house. Every day there was cleanliness and godliness as she washed, dusted, swept and cooked before work, where she would do the same thing on a grander scale. In the evening she read the newspapers and then her Bible. At the weekend she helped clean the church she had helped build on Sans Souci Hill. On the first of every month she put one hundred dollars in an envelope and told Trevor to give it to his Uncle. She could only be grateful for the house he had given her ever since Trevor's father, Harry Beharry, left for Canada to look for work and a better life. Before Harry left sixteen years ago, he promised *his doudou* he would send for her and their baby boy once he was 'set up nice'.

When he left, Louise and Trevor were still living in a room that Harry's family had built at the back of his mother's chicken farm in Carapichaima. The dark room with its cold, damp, concrete floor was infested with mosquitoes and filled with the smell of rotting chicken guts. No matter how often Louise sprayed the room with her watery perfume, the smell stayed in their clothes, the bed, the curtains; she even smelt it on her baby's skin. Since Trevor's birth, she had begged Harry to cover the floor and ask his mother to dump the chicken guts lower down the river. Every Monday morning, before Harry left for work at his cousin's tyre shop, he promised to put down a linoleum mat and talk to Ma about the chicken guts. But he never did.

One day, Louise, unable to spend another day without a mat and with that stink smell, found herself in Ma's house. Ma had never liked Louise, ashamed that her first son had brought home a Negro wife with a belly and that her first grandchild was a blue-black half-breed *dougla*. Ma had had dreams of her Harry and Camilla Singh – 'such a nice Hindu girl, good family and thing.' So when Louise dared to ask Ma for a mat, Ma told her plain she should be happy with what she had, especially since she wasn't still in that nasty building in town doing all her jamette business in the bar downstairs. Ma knew that Harry and other men from the village were regulars at the bar where Louise was a waitress or dancer, depending on the clientele. Harry asked her to leave the bar and follow him to the country. So Louise left her life of sin in Port-of-Spain and found God in Carapichaima.

Three months turned to six and Harry never sent for them. 'Your father made promises he couldn't keep,' was all Miss Louise would say on the few occasions that Trevor asked about his father. But Trevor knew from his Auntie Patsy, Uncle Patrick's common-law wife, that his father was 'set up nice in foreign with a house, a white lady-friend and plenty children.' Still Louise, for whatever reason, acted like a respectful Hindu widow who had seen her husband's body wrapped in white muslin and burnt to ashes on a pyre on the banks of the Caroni River.

When Trevor came back from Mr Taylor, his mother was

already at home. She sat on the front steps, clutching her bag and the newspapers. Trevor opened the front door and carried her heavy brown-paper bag full of oranges from the Pierres into the house. He didn't want to talk about the lesson with Mr Taylor and his mother was too exhausted to ask for more than 'It was OK?'

After dinner Trevor washed the dishes and put them away while Miss Louise sat in her favourite chair, mouthing the passage from the Bible she was reading. She had had Trevor at seventeen, Trevor's age now, and had started to work in the bar at thirteen, having left home at twelve to move in with her mother's sister. Her mother never tried to bring her back to the house because she claimed that 'Louise was causing too much confusion.' But the only confusion, both mother and daughter knew, was that 'Uncle' Stevie, her mother's friend, liked to barge into Louise's bedroom when she was undressing. The room had a curtain but no door. One night he crept next to her bed with a torchlight and tried to pull up her nightgown. Louise screamed, Uncle Stevie slapped her mouth and then left the room. The next morning she begged her mother to move in with her aunt. Her brother Patrick, who also hated Uncle Stevie, had already left.

Miss Louise wasn't old but she looked old, she moved old, she talked old and she dressed old. She didn't drink. Trevor had never seen her dance. She had a ticklish laugh but Trevor seldom heard it. Her forehead was lined from a perpetual frown. She was probably the same age as Mrs Pierre, and much younger than Uncle Patrick, but they all treated her like their Miss Louise, and she didn't seem to mind. Her life was to 'serve the Almighty and the Pierres,' Uncle Patrick would always say.

On Sundays, Trevor woke up before the sunrise, tiptoed around the house on the sandy grains of their termite infested floors, and tried his best not to disturb his mother who slept until seven on her Sabbath. Out in the yard he pushed his bike past his uncle's pot hounds. Closing the gate behind him, he rode away from Sans Souci and its Sunday morning odours from the Saturday night limes that left the pavements stinking of stale beer, rum and urine. Across the bridge, the one his mother crossed every morning, he rode past the Pierres' neighbourhood with the fortress walls and long driveways lined with bougainvillea and fishtail palms. From then on it was up the hill, past Mary's 'I am the Way, the Truth and the Light Mini Mart', through the bamboo canopy, over the Saddle and into a valley called Orange Vale, not because the valley was full of oranges, but because in the dry season flowering immortelle trees lined the road and set fire to the hills with their flowers. Further into the valley were cocoa estates and fields of watermelon, pawpaw and pineapple. He met his riding buddies, Nigel and Jules, just beyond the last cocoa plantation in Orange Vale, outside the gate of one of the horse farms. They had all gone to the same overcrowded Senior Sec., but had said little to each other then. It was not until they met on the trails in the Valley that they became friends.

This was the first time since Trevor got his third-hand bike two years ago (a Christmas gift from Miss Louise) that he was going to enter a race. Nigel and Jules had convinced him that he took the hills better than both of them so he stood the best chance against all the top mountain-bike riders on the island. They promised to help Trevor with the registration fee of one hundred dollars and share in the spoils when Trevor took home the trophy and one thousand dollars. Although Trevor had never won anything in his life, he agreed.

That morning, a week before the Pine Hill Race the following Sunday, he knew he had to beat Pine Hill, something none of them had been able to do without a fall. When they got to the bottom of the trail for the race, they stopped to eat some pomeracs. Most of the fruit, shrivelled and a deep burgundy, had fallen to the ground, filling the air with tiny fruit flies and the smell of strong pomerac wine.

Riding the trail, they talked about the way Trevor should handle the race route. Jules said that technique mattered more than the fancy bikes the rich boys had, but all Trevor could think about was making it, fall-free, down Pine Hill. Finally at the top, Nigel and Jules positioned themselves on either side of Trevor.

'Find your line, see the thing in your mind and go brave, man.'

Trevor said a quick prayer, then released his pull on the brakes and headed down the hill at full speed. But the descent was too sudden to stop the old fears from coming back; he lost his line, zigzagged and pulled too hard on his front brakes to avoid a pine-tree trunk. Trevor lost control and flew over his handlebars, just missing the tree trunk but still landing with a thump on the ground. He rolled over a few times and stopped just short of the riverbed. He lay there on his back, in pain, in shock, drifting, in and out of a dream about riding through groves of immortelle trees whose orange flowers became butterflies as they fell from the branches. When next Trevor opened his eyes he was in bed with his mother on one side and Dr Singh on the other. Heads popped up and down outside his window, accompanied by shrieks and giggles from his cousins.

Before Dr Singh left, he told Miss Louise that Trevor just needed time to rest and heal, but she still looked worried.

'Don't worry, Ma, everything will be OK.' Trevor held his mother's hands and kissed both palms; her church had taught her to forgive everyone but herself.

The following Sunday, Nigel and Jules rode up to Trevor's gate. Miss Louise was inside, preparing the usual Sunday lunch feast of callaloo, macaroni pie, rice and stewed chicken. Trevor was sitting outside under the sapodilla tree with his leg in a cast stretched out on a stool. She looked at him through the glass louvres, happy to see her son with his 'face in a book'. Since Trevor could not come to the Tuesday lesson, Mr Taylor arrived bearing gifts in a shopping bag. While Trevor was 'indisposed', he thought he could 'amuse himself with a few of his friends'. Thinking it had to do with war or maybe his own life, *The Waste Land* immediately caught Trevor's attention. Barking dogs woke him up from his trance and he hobbled to the gate on his crutches. Jules kept riding up to the gate teasing the dogs. Trevor shooed them away with one of his crutches.

'Like you barely mobile, boy,' Jules said holding out his clenched fist for a bounce.

'Yeah boy, I have another three weeks in this thing.' Trevor pointed to this cast. One of the braver pot hounds made its way back to the gate; this time Trevor hit its bony back with his crutch. It squealed and ran to the back of the yard.

'You missed a great race, boy,' Nigel said.

'You mean you missed some great falls. The only one who took the hill like a boss was Hakim. The rest of them walk down, take it real slow or try to take it fast and end up on their backside.' Jules mimicked a fall, shifting his bike from left to right, then pretended to topple over the handlebar.

'So you enter the race or what?' Trevor asked Jules.

'No boy,' Nigel replied. 'Like Jules take that fall harder than you, boy, he ain't even sign up for the thing.' They all laughed.

Just then his Uncle Patrick pulled up to the gate in his taxi full of his screaming children. Every Sunday, stale drunk or not, he took the family to their church, just above Trevor's mother's church on Sans Souci Hill. Nigel opened the gate for the car. Uncle Patrick, with his usual hangover frown, barely acknowledged Trevor or his friends.

'So your boss son win again, boy,' said Jules.

'Not my boss, boy, they find somebody else already. Say what, easy come, easy go.' Trevor forced a smile, hoping it could cover how much he knew his mother counted on the ends he brought home every month from the Pharmacy.

'So what you doing now?' Nigel asked. Mr Taylor and the books crossed his mind but he said, 'Nothing boy, just waiting for this thing to come off and take a ride.' They all nodded.

'Well we making a turn, heading up to the Orange today. Later.' They rode off and Trevor stared at them until they turned the bend at the stream.

KITE SEASON

Kite Season

This is what I remember. A mid-morning at our home in the valley, my brother, who has just turned ten, runs across the lawn, trying to fly a birthday kite. The dogs follow him. The sky is a blinding white, flowers from the immortelle tree spread an orange carpet on the grass, my father is picking grapefruits from the trees along the fence, my mother is sitting on the porch reading, and I am trying to catch the kite's tail as the breeze makes it dance in the air.

At the dinner table my brother and I are teasing each other about things in school: a boy who likes me, a girl who likes him. My mother sips her red wine, my father doesn't seem to hear, and then suddenly my brother says something very funny and we both start to laugh; my mother laughs too, my father gives a rare smile. What the joke was I can't recall, but it doesn't matter. What does matter is the laughter that rises above the table and floats like my brother's kite.

At school-break time those two boys are teasing me again about my plaits that stick up in the air, my legs that look like dry twigs, my eyes that are too wide for my face, my nose that is too small, and my full-moon head that is too big for my skinny body. My throat hurts from trying so hard not to cry but then the tears start to flow and the boys laugh for everyone to hear. That night I tell my brother about the boys. My brother says I shouldn't be such a cry baby, but the next day in school I see my brother and his friends surround the two boys; they form a circle around them so I can't hear what they say, but those boys never tease me again.

We are lying in bed, my brother on the top bunk, I on the lower. It is deep night. Our parents are arguing; my father's voice sounds like someone is strangling him and my mother shouts, then shushes. We cannot hear the words but their muffled sounds remind us of American movies we see on TV. All parents argue, my brother says as he comes down to the lower bunk and lies next to me. We fall asleep again before the noises stop.

On vacation with our cousins my brother avoids me even though he knows I prefer to be around the boys more than the girls. But when they search for crabs in the rocks, or buried sand dollars, or sticks along the beach, my brother chases me away like a stray dog. He sends me to play with my girl cousin, Sarah, who prefers to look pretty on a beach towel rather than run with the boys. My father sees that I am unhappy so he takes me into the sea and we body-surf the waves all the way to the shore. Before long, my brother and cousins join us. I learn right then that laughter is the best revenge.

The day of Common Entrance results: on the island all the children have to take this exam at ten, eleven or twelve to try to get into the best high schools; there are too many children and not enough good schools so they have to make the exam very hard in order to separate the sheep from the goats. That is what they say to us in school but I can never decide if I want to be a sheep or a goat; neither choice seems pleasant. My brother has been nervous all week, hitting me and teasing me even more than normal. One night I even hear him cry while my mother says prayers in his room. I feel sorry for him; he is so smart but gets nervous about his tests. My mother is anxious; she snaps at us for the smallest things; my father looks sterner than he usually does. The house has a strange feeling like something big is about to happen. Whatever happens I don't want to see my brother cry; at times I hate him but I hate to see him cry even more.

Sins

This is what I remember from the first day of high school. My father walks me into the main office, gives my name to an old English lady, who then passes me along to a prefect for a quick tour of the school compound before we get to my classroom. Everything about the prefect is neat: her thick long plait, her very white socks, the bows on her black sneakers, her starched white shirt, ironed navy skirt, ironed red tie, and most of all her sentences. They are neat, never too long or too short. 'This is the lower school bathroom.' 'This is Miss McCarthy's tuck shop.' 'The library is open from 7 a.m. to 4 p.m. and at lunch.' 'You will learn how to use the library during library hour.' 'Never leave the school premises during school hours.' 'To leave you need a handwritten excuse from a parent or guardian.' 'This is the tennis court.' 'That is the chapel.' She is perfect, a perfect prefect. After my tour I abandon all hope of ever being perfect or a prefect.

In high school I observe two ways to know if a boy likes you. The first is called Tobago Love; this is when the boy will try to hurt the girl through words or actions but deep inside he worships the ground the girl walks on. The other way is Movie Town Love where the boy bravely displays how much he likes the girl in front of everyone. Where I come from this second option is not a common practice, and furthermore in my high school there are only girls. So our experience of boys is very limited, at least in the lower forms, so these types of love, Tobago and Movie Town, remain for the most part just ideas.

In high school we learn a lot about sin, mainly from our priest Father Blackburn. He is white, looks much older than a hundred and fifty, and his face and hands are full of brown, liver spots. Father Blackburn's back is bent, his hair is thick, parted to one side and very white, his eyelids are like umbrellas over his light blue eyes, but he is not a bad man, as the other girls like to say, only an Englishman, and that shouldn't be a sin. We see Father Blackburn twice a week besides Morning Assembly prayers and Chapel for RI (Religious Instruction). Often our vice principal,

Ms Lyla, will sit and listen to his instructions. She makes sure he never strays too far away from her favourite subject – sin. In fact his main purpose is to teach us that we are sinners. We are born into sin, we are all sinners; our goal in life should be to do enough good so that it outweighs our sins. I do not need Father Blackburn to know I am a sinner and a liar. Sins are committed in thoughts, words and deeds. So I am definitely a sinner and most sinners are liars. I have stolen a chocolate bar from Miss McCarthy's tuck shop. I have taken a sharp stone and scraped Ms Lyla's red car. Even if I have never called Shireen a stupid coolie, I have thought it; the same for Merlana, who I think looks like a fat black gorilla; and every day of my year in form one I have envied Katie's straight, blond hair. I have imagined a slow, painful death for Ms McGreggor, our English Literature teacher. In my mind I have tongue-kissed Mr French, our Algebra teacher, and I am even more in love with Mr Samuel, the grounds' keeper.

In high school is when I attend my first Hindu funeral. The man was a friend of my father's. Or should I say *is* a friend of my father's? Are they still friends even though he is dead? They knew each other since high school. So I attend the funeral with my mother and father; my brother has an end of term exam he cannot miss. We drive for weeks and months until we get to the house where the ceremony will take place under a white galvanized shed at the back of a small house. I have never been to this part of the country before. I have never seen so many *roti* shops and doubles stands. My father wears a black suit, my mother a black dress and I am in my school uniform. When we enter I notice that all the Indian people are in white. White is for weddings, white is also for funerals. My father's friend has (or had?) two tall beautiful daughters, who talk about their father, who sing the calypsos he wrote, who tell us about his love of India and his love of cricket and carnival. After the prayers, they put garlands on the body. My father's friend has been lying there, listening to what is being said about him. I wonder how he feels? Or if he actually agrees? We drive for ten more years before we get to a place called the Temple in the Sea, which is not a lie because the temple is actually in the

sea, not far out, close to the shore, but in the sea nevertheless. This
is where they burn the bodies on a pyre. They cover it with blocks
of white pine, with at least four buckets of soft ghee; they sprinkle
the body with brown sugar and slide it into the neat pile of wood,
like a loaf of sweet bread sliding into an oven. Other bodies burn
on the pyres all round us. The fires are bright orange. It is windy
so the wind blows the black smoke towards the sea. When the fire
starts I see a black outline of the face. Orange and black are the
colours I remember just before I hear the skull go pop!

In high school my mother didn't do very well and she is afraid
that my brother and I will do the same. So she terrorizes us when
exam time comes around. She screams all the time, my father hides
himself in the garden, and my brother and I are prisoners of her
forever-changing moods. Inevitably we disappoint her; my brother
struggles to keep his Bs and I never move beyond a B+. I know with
just a little more work I can get that A she so craves but I do not make
the extra effort. I do this on purpose; that way I can get back at my
mother for all the hardships we have endured. But my brother tries
hard to please her and fails at every attempt. All his sad attempts
make me livid and I tell him not to try so hard. Easy for you, he
always says, at least you have Daddy on your side. So he tries not to
disappoint her but inevitably he does and must then face the
punishment for disappointing our mother; first there is silence but
only after she screams and shouts at us for ten hours; then she will
stop talking altogether. We only receive instructions about what is
absolutely necessary: 'Breakfast is on the table,' 'Dinner is ready,'
'Take a shower,' 'Get ready.' And we are left to say prayers without
her. She makes it quite clear that her love has been taken away, held
hostage until the mood subsides or until the grades improve.

In high school we spend most of the long summer vacation
time at the seaside. My mother's family own three houses on
three acres of land; the three siblings will inherit a house each
when my mother's parents die. My mother has an older sister,
Aunt Claire, and a younger brother, Bobby. They are never all on
the property together; even when Bobby comes home to visit
from Italy where he says he lives with a beautiful Italian wife,

whom no one has ever seen. At night I hear the waves crash against the rocks because the house my mother will inherit is built very close to the cliff overlooking the Atlantic Ocean; the water is a dark blue, not like on the other side of the island where the Caribbean Sea is a much lighter green. We swim at our private beach in the morning, but after lunch we go to the beach below the lighthouse. At the lighthouse beach (this is our family name for the beach, the villagers call it Espérance) the Caribbean and the Atlantic meet and my brother thinks he knows the exact spot, just beyond a huge rock. My favourite place when we are at the sea is below the lighthouse facing that rock where the Caribbean and Atlantic meet. This is where I dream my dreams of becoming a famous painter or writer or singer. My brother and cousins try to fish off the edge of the lighthouse cliff, not far from where I sit. But the water is too rough; it hits the rocks hard and splashes into their faces. I can feel a spray from where I am. Only the pelicans can catch fish here; they dive, open their deep beaks, and scoop up thousands of tiny fish. The sea gulls fly just above the pelicans.

I remember one morning waking up very early with my brother and going down the stairs for a glass of water; at the bottom of the stairs all the rooms look as though they are filled with a powdery pink-and-orange mist; we can smell the rain and the sea even though we are far away from the beach. Our parents' voices had us awake all night. They have been arguing for weeks, for years, but now they try to hide it from us, especially my mother, who tries to be very cheerful the morning after a row. She thinks we haven't heard but we have. My brother and I are used to this now, her fake smiles and extra hugs. We prefer it when she is herself, grumpy, ordering us around like soldiers, or maybe I should say *I* prefer it, since my brother seems to like it that she doesn't care about his Spanish grade and that he's been getting detentions almost daily.

In high school, in my final year, my parents get a divorce. No, that is not quite true; in my final year of high school, in the middle of my A-Level exams, my parents announce their desire to separate. They separate, not divorce, and then we live through a period of back and forth, of never knowing which separation will last forever. My brother and I have been expecting this separation since birth; we are not really surprised; we know they are opposites, never agreeing, always arguing, this way never that way, up not down, here not there, fire and water, not meant to last beyond the expiry date on the wedding cake. And yet they say to us that they will always love each other. Love: this mysterious word that hides so many sins. My brother tries to comfort my mother even though my father is the one in real pain. I take no sides, or at least I try not to blame my mother. In high school I hate them both but I hate my A-Level exams even more. And so I spend all my time in the library; all I want to do is find a way to get out. And I do.

Away

This is what I remember. Escaping from my home is not difficult; in fact I am encouraged by both sides to leave. My father tells me all about his life on campus; he studied, no 'read', Politics, Philosophy and Economics. My mother never went away to university, so instead of stories of her studies she buys me sweaters and jackets. My brother is the only one who truly looks sad to see me go; he knows this is the last time we will share our stories; once I am away everything will change. I will be replaced and so will he. My father travels with me to Boston; he is there for my orientation and registration; he helps me settle into my dorm room. My mother arrives the day after my father leaves and buys me things for my dorm room: a desk lamp, a comforter, cushions, sheets, towels, a new computer, more sweaters and toiletries to last a semester.

I live on the International Floor with other Internationals and Americans who want to live with Internationals. I am the only one from the Caribbean on my floor: there are Venezuelans there to learn English, some Japanese, some French girls, and four Moslem girls from Malaysia whose perfectly round faces are the only things we see. They put me in a room with one of these girls; we live together for three weeks before all the Malaysian Moslem girls ask to be put on another floor. The International floor is not for them. With the loud music, with the Venezuelan boys trying to pick up the blond American girls, with the Japanese boys falling for the French, with the American boy Andy doing cocaine on a huge mirror, with Claire trying to convert us all to her American Christianity, who can blame the Malaysian girls for leaving.

I do not feel at home in this city, Boston; I am alone in so many ways: the only black girl in most of my classes, even though at home no one would call me black; the only black girl at the table where we have lunch in the university dining halls. At home they say my family is mixed, not black; at home Merlana is black; at home some people might even call my father's family white; and my mother's family is part-Chinese, part-Portuguese and part-African, but no one on her side would ever say they were black. But black is what they call me here, and black is what they might call most of my family as well. So the black American students invite me to sit with them at their table even though I feel even more alone there; their table is on the edge of the hall, it is like a boat in the middle of an ocean of white. I cannot be comfortable in this city, where everything is grey: the buildings, the people, the walkways, even the snow. I will never feel at home in this place called Boston.

The winters are depressing, dark when I wake up, and dark when I get out of classes. The wind from the Charles River can lift you off your feet and make your nose feel as though it will freeze and drop right off. But close to the river is where I like to walk, especially when is it completely frozen and the whiteness can be beautifully strange. I fall in love three times walking along the Charles: with a Frank, a Pierre and a John. All English majors like me, except for Pierre who was majoring in History. These loves don't hurt, they come and go, fall to winter, winter to spring, and so on. I do not want to remember much about these loves along the river. I make no ties in this city; I know it is just a place for me to be away.

Home

This is what I remember. My mother, not my father who usually comes for me when I have a late flight, meets me at the airport; she stands at the exit with an anxious look on her face until she sees me and then smiles her beautiful wide smile. We hug but I do not remember her being so small. She looks as though she has shrunk since I saw her at Christmas. There is wonderful news since last I was at home, she says, with a nervous smile; my father has returned and come back after so many years, but I know they will not last. We are used to this back and forth, my brother and I, no longer trusting anything they say to us. I only remember the blackness of this night, no stars; I remember passing the billboards on the highway; I do not remember what my mother says to me about herself and my father. But I remember that there is no moon, only some grey clouds that move fast across the night sky and this means rain. I am home, home for good, but I do not feel anything special. My mother, my brother and my father are all at the house to greet me. My room is the same, the house has the same smells, and I lie in my bed; but before I fall asleep on my first night I remember a mid-morning at our home in the valley. My brother, who has just turned ten, runs across the lawn trying to fly a birthday kite; the dogs follow him, my mother is reading, my father is in the yard picking fruit and I can see myself at the lighthouse making wishes that disappear like the kite into that blinding white sky.

ABOUT THE AUTHOR

Elizabeth Walcott-Hackshaw is a Senior Lecturer in French and Francophone Literatures in the Department of Modern Languages and Linguistics, The University of the West Indies, St Augustine, Trinidad and Tobago.

Her publications include *Border Crossings: A Trilingual Anthology of Caribbean Women Writers* (2012), co-edited with Nicole Roberts, *Echoes of the Haitian Revolution 1804-2004* (2008) and *Reinterpreting the Haitian Revolution and its Cultural Aftershocks* (1804-2004) (2006) co-edited with Martin Munro. *Four Taxis Facing North*, her first collection of short stories, was translated into Italian in 2010 by Giuseppe Sofo.

She left Trinidad at eighteen years old to study at Boston University where she received a BA degree in French and English, followed by a Masters and PhD in French. Her first short story was published in 1987 whilst studying in Boston. In 1992 she returned to Trinidad, where she lives with her husband and two teenage children. Her father is the Nobel Prize for Literature winning writer Derek Walcott. She has taught French and Franco-Caribbean Literature at the University of the West Indies, and is presently the Deputy Dean of Graduate Studies and Research in the Faculty of Humanities and Education where she continues to lecture on French Caribbean Literature.

Mrs. B.
ISBN: 9781845232313; pp. 194; pub. 2014; price: £9.99

Ruthie's academic success has been Mrs. B's pride and joy, but as the novel begins, she and her husband Charles are on their way to the airport to collect their daughter who has had a nervous breakdown after an affair with a married professor.

Loosely inspired by Flaubert's *Madame Bovary*, *Mrs. B* focuses on the life of an upper middle-class family in contemporary Trinidad, who have, in response to the island's crime and violence, retreated to a gated community. Mrs. B (she hates the name of Butcher) is fast approaching fifty and her daughter Ruthie's return from university and the state of her marriage provoke her to some unaccustomed self-reflection. Like Flaubert's heroine Mrs. B's desires are often tied to the expectations of her social circle.

Elizabeth Walcott-Hackshaw writes with wit, with brutal honesty and with warmth for her characters, but the novel questions how far the Butcher clan's love of Trinidad as place – their hedonistic pleasure in their holiday houses "down the islands" – can carry them towards a deeper engagement with their fellow but less privileged islanders.

"...richly entertaining. Walcott-Hackshaw offers a vigorous, at times sizzling, prose that is grounded in local rhythms and allusions to the culture that is at once both the object of her love and also her main target."

Arnold Rampersad, *Trinidad Guardian*

★Available in print and e-book★